S0-BHR-234

GO AND BURY YOUR DEAD

Center Point
Large Print

Also by Bill Brooks and available from
Center Point Large Print:

Vengeance Trail
Frontier Justice
Ride the Man Down
Men of Violence

GO AND BURY YOUR DEAD

A JOHN HENRY COLE STORY

Bill Brooks

CENTER POINT LARGE PRINT
THORNDIKE, MAINE

This Center Point Large Print edition
is published in the year 2018 by arrangement with
Golden West Literary Agency.

Copyright © 2014 by Bill Brooks.

All rights reserved.

The text of this Large Print edition is unabridged.
In other aspects, this book may vary
from the original edition.
Printed in the United States of America
on permanent paper.
Set in 16-point Times New Roman type.

ISBN: 978-1-68324-896-5 (hardcover)
ISBN: 978-1-68324-900-9 (paperback)

Library of Congress Cataloging-in-Publication Data

Names: Brooks, Bill, 1943- author.
Title: Go and bury your dead : a John Henry Cole story / Bill Brooks.
Description: Center Point Large Print edition. | Thorndike, Maine :
    Center Point Large Print, 2018.
Identifiers: LCCN 2018019218| ISBN 9781683248965 (hardcover :
    alk. paper) | ISBN 9781683249009 (paperback : alk. paper)
Subjects: LCSH: Ranchers—Fiction. | Kidnapping victims—Fiction. |
    Outlaws—Fiction. | Large type books. | GSAFD: Western stories.
Classification: LCC PS3552.R65863 G6 2018 | DDC 813/.54—dc23
LC record available at https://lccn.loc.gov/2018019218

GO AND BURY
YOUR DEAD

CHAPTER ONE

The Pinkerton and the killer sat across from each other at a back table in Karl's Liberty Palace Saloon on a quiet Sunday morning with only the company of a barkeeper fat as a bulldog who slept atop a billiard table. And then there was the woman with platinum hair.

In the distance they could hear the lone church's bell hesitant gong drawing forth a straggling small group of folks—men in black coats and hats, women in skirts with muddied hems towing reluctant children with sad faces. Not many, but more than expected for a place such as this.

Otherwise, the outer world of Gun Town was quiet, the whores all still asleep in their trundle beds within the walls of small cribs, those walls papered with yellow and curled newspapers and catalog pages for insulation more than reading among the mostly illiterate flesh. Usually in a corner was a washstand with a basin of fetid water, the languid air still smelling of sweat and sexual musk, cigar smoke, stale liquor, and hopelessness.

At the opposite end of town from the church stood the tent city that was temporary home to gunfighters, pimps, gamblers, luckless prospectors, and saddle tramps on the drift—a moveable feast of humanity as the local and lone town official referred to it. He was the washed-up end of the line of a lawman named Bill Hammer. He used to be a man to be reckoned with in the old days, but no longer. He kept out of the way and put on a good face and sometimes arrested drunks, and sometimes not.

All along the main drag the doors of any sort of honest business were locked, awnings of white and green stripes rolled up, *CLOSED* signs hung in windows with the husks of dead flies adorning their sills. Sunday was for praying, for rest, for shutting down—all but the saloons and cathouses and gambling parlors. The morning itself was bright and clear as a polished whiskey glass, the sky as blue as a gas flame. The weather held promise of something other than snow or rain. It held promise of beauty, a rare thing in Gun Town.

Down at the telegraph office the telegrapher slept with his head on his forearms, his key silent for once, the old man glad for the relief, his shoes unlaced and kicked off, a hole in one sock that let a big toe poke out. Up at the livery the liveryman slept in a bed of straw in an unoccupied stall, the sweet warm milky scent of a brood mare and her colt in the next stall. He had a swollen lip from the night before when he'd gotten into an altercation with a big teamster over Maggie O'Berne, a whore with two differently colored eyes, fat as a blue shoat hog. She said she could handle them both at once if they agreed, but that is what started the fight. The teamster suggested the liveryman could wait his turn and the liveryman objected, braved up by the rot-gut whiskey he'd been drinking since noon. But the teamster wasn't to be denied. The blow of his fist drove the liveryman's lower tooth through his lip that spilled blood as if he'd been swiped by a straight razor.

"You bring the money?" Lucky Jack said.

"I have access to it," replied the Pinkerton.

"What's that supposed to mean . . . access? You got it, don't you?"

"I just have to make a few things happen and it's yours."

Lucky Jack wasn't the killer's real name; it was Jack Dancer. He may have gotten the nickname Lucky because of his shock of hair that was the color of maple leaves in late autumn, or, some said, the flames of the fire that burned down the Rincon Hotel in Lead, Colorado that time when Dancer was marshal there and suspected of keeping a second job as arsonist for hire.

"Then let's see it."

"It's not as simple as that."

"It needs to be as simple as that. Straight up deal. The only way I like to do business."

"I don't think so."

"Why don't you think so? You want her back,

right? Take her home to her husband, ain't that why you're here?"

"That's the plan."

The Pinkerton's name was Charley Cisco. He carried a pair of matching bulldog revolvers in special pockets sewn into his linen duster. He had the weathered features of a scrub pine and the eyes of a wolf. His voice was like gravel crunched under iron wheels.

"Then you'll need to show me the money."

"Soon as I have the girl in hand."

"She sits right there," Lucky Jack said. He seemed more amused by the negotiations than troubled.

"They treat you all right, miss?" the Pinkerton said, turning to the woman.

The woman nodded.

She was even prettier than her tintype and much younger than the man who'd hired the detective to get her back. It was of no great wonder to the Pinkerton; many older men, widowed men of holdings, married younger women once their wives died. But still, she was a looker, this Lenora Wilson.

"Here's how it's going to work," Charley Cisco said. "She and I are going to walk out of here and get on the next cannonball heading south, and soon as that happens I'll wire the bank here in town to release the money to you. It's already there, just waiting for my word to release it."

"And what if you decide not to release it and the pair of you are already halfway to Cheyenne, then how's it work, detective?"

"Do I seem to you the sort of man who would play games with you, Lucky, knowing your reputation? I came here alone, not with a posse of men or a storm of detectives. That should show you something about my intentions to do the right thing here, and also about Mister Wilson's intentions. He just wants his wife back. The money isn't important to him."

Lucky Jack groomed his heavy mustaches with his thumb and forefinger. "You forgetting the bank is closed Sundays?"

"I've made special arrangements with Mister Timmons, the president, to await my word. He will come in and release the money to you once I wire him at the next station."

"Then go on and take her, detective. But if you cross me, I'll make you pray to Jesus that I kill you before I'm finished with you."

The Pinkerton nodded, rose from his chair, and said: "Miss, you come along with me now. Your husband is anxiously waiting your return."

She stood, cast one last look at her kidnapper, and turned and walked out with the detective.

"I've a room over at the hotel," he said. "Some fresh clothes for you that your husband sent along. You can freshen up while we wait for the cannonball."

She followed obediently, in silence.

In the room she saw a dress of blue organdy laid out across the bed, a folded stack of under-garments next to it, stockings and a pair of gray button-up shoes at the foot of the bed.

There was a side table with wash basin and pitcher decorated with dancing nymphs and a large copper tub of soapy water in front of the window that let in morning light turning the bubbles iridescent.

"I had the bath brought up for you, figuring you might enjoy it," the Pinkerton said.

"How thoughtful of you, detective."

"I'll just go send a wire to your husband to let him know you're now in my care, then I'll wait for you in the lobby," Charley Cisco said. "Let you have a bit of privacy, after . . ." He didn't need to finish it.

She stripped out of her clothes and lowered herself into the warm bath, closing her eyes as she submerged, a sigh escaping her smiling lips.

Oh what tangled webs we weave, she thought.

Charley Cisco exited the hotel and crossed over to where the telegraph office was, the streets still vacant but for one lonesome cowpuncher heading back to his ranch with a snoot full of tanglefoot and empty pockets, a weekend shot and another month till pay day.

Charley did not see the two men watching him from up the street, their hat brims pulled low over their feral eyes, the way they slouched as they leaned against support posts in front of a hardware store housing blankets and muskrat traps, saw blades and hammers, and cold cast-iron pump handles.

"That him?" Spade asked the other man.

"That's him," Gypsy Flynn said.

"Take him now, or wait?"

"Let him send his wire, then we'll take him."

"What if we can't make him give Lucky what he wants . . . I mean what if we kill him accidental in the trying?"

"We won't kill him," Gypsy said. He was a man who spoke out of the side of his mouth as though everything he said was some low secret. "I know how to do it."

"It'll be fun to learn from the best."

"Not for him it won't."

Spade leaned forward and spat a brown stream into the street and brushed his whiskered mouth with his wrist. "What about her?" he said, looking toward the hotel's upper windows.

"We'll retrieve her after we finish the job."

"A bird in the hand, huh?"

"Something like that," Gypsy said, his eyes full of a hunger that food or drink couldn't fix.

The Pinkerton exited the telegraph office again, and walked to the train depot located on the same side of the street as the two men who were watching him.

"Let's shake a leg," Gypsy said. "Remember what you're supposed to do."

"I remember."

Charley Cisco bought two tickets on the cannonball due in at quarter past noon and stuck them in his hatband, then went out again. A man stood there with an unlit cigarette.

"Pardon, you wouldn't have a match on you would you, mister?"

Cisco reached inside his shirt pocket where he always kept a spare Blue Diamond or two he used for toothpicks, and took one out. "Here you go."

Then he felt the cold press of steel just behind his ear.

"Smoking's a nasty habit, or ain't you heard?" a voice from behind the gun said.

"You boys are about to rob a poor man," Cisco said. "What I've got is fifteen dollars and some Indian head pennies, but you're welcome to them."

"I don't think so," Gypsy said from behind. "Now just walk into that alley yonder and don't kick up a fuss unless you want your mama to get a letter saying as how you was murdered."

"She'd sure hate the hell out of that," the Pinkerton said, leading on toward the alley.

"You go stay with the woman," Gypsy said to Spade, "and if she kicks up a fuss, cut her throat while I shoot this one. Or, if I'm not back in ten minutes, cut her throat anyway."

"Can I have my pleasure with her first?"

"Only after you kill her, Spade. That's about the onliest way you'd get a woman to diddle with you." Once Spade left, Gypsy said: "Here's how it's gonna work. You and me are gonna march back in that telegraph office and have that old cross-eyed fool inside run a message over to the banker to release the money to Lucky. If you hesitate, put up a squawk, or do anything stupid, that weasel who was just here is going to kill that ol' boy's woman and you'll end belly in the creek like a speared carp. We clear?"

"We're clear."

"Now let me relieve you of them bulldog pistols."

When it was finished and the Pinkerton did as ordered, the two men stepped out again and waited until the telegrapher carried the wire down the street toward the church where the telegrapher said was where he'd find Mr. Timmons.

Just then the First Free Will Methodist Church at the opposite end of town had ended its services and the congregants were emerging and lingering in the broad yard, shaking hands with the preacher. An ice cream social was planned for later, the preacher exhorting: "We might be small in number but large in fellowship."

"Ain't that a swell sight," Gypsy said as he waited until he saw the telegrapher hand the banker the paper, saw the banker look up, shake his head, and say something to the messenger.

The telegrapher came back and said to Gypsy: "Mister Timmons said he don't know anything about what it says in that message."

"That so? Move on out, detective!"

Then he marched the Pinkerton back down the alley and up behind the store fronts where a pair of saddle horses were tied up.

"Me and you are going to take a little ride," Gypsy said. "Get on that flea bag."

Mounted, Gypsy led the Pinkerton to a spot along a creek lined by willows and old cotton-woods, the town still in view but at a distance.

"Get down off your horse," the gunman ordered.

All the while Charley Cisco was trying to figure a way to get the jump on this miscreant but so far there hadn't been an opening and it was starting to look like he might be forced to do something desperate or face dying in a lonely place.

"Now put your arms up."

The Pinkerton did as ordered while the gunman pressed the barrel of his revolver to the back of the Pinkerton's neck and with the other hand patted him down.

"Well, now, what's this? Feels like a money belt, don't it? Why, by God, it is a money belt. Take it off and drop it in the grass. Now the watch and chain. Drop them, too."

Charlie did so. "Let me ask you something," he

said over his shoulder. "How is it you walk like a damned duck?"

Gypsy's face clouded with anger, being sensitive about his deformed limp. It might be his only chance, Charlie thought, to get the damned fool off guard, by getting him mad, making him do something stupid like swing on him.

"Turn around so I can shoot you in your damn' face!"

"You kill me and you'll bring down the weight of the law on you," Charlie said, but even he knew it to be a weak bluff. Still he would not turn around.

He heard the clicking of the revolver's mechanism as the hammer was thumbed back, turning the cylinder, felt the gunman's hot rotten breath on the back of his neck.

"Shooting you would be as easy as killing a baby," Gypsy said. "I don't want it to be that easy, Pinkerton man. Now you fooled old Lucky back there with your bullshit story, but you couldn't fool me. Now I got the money and you got nothing but a prayer left you. How's it feel to be so high and mighty now?"

"Let's say I had a lot more money than what's in that money belt I could get my hands on? You interested?"

"Well, now, that's a right good question. But I know a flannel mouth when I hear one. So here's an answer for you."

17

Then something sharp and electrifying punched Charlie Cisco in the back just where his right kidney rode and his entire body knotted in rebellious agony. In spite of himself he cried out: "Oh, God!" Then once, twice, three times more the punching pain shot through him and caused him to collapse to his knees where he kneeled gasping, then slowly twisted onto his side, his knees drawn up, and looking up into the hot glare of sun and sky and the shadow of a killer over him. Through squinted eyes the detective saw the flash of bloody blade in Gypsy's left hand, his cocked revolver in his right hand.

"Too easy to shoot you, Pinkerton. This is better. This is the way I like to do it . . . slow and painful-like."

Charlie Cisco's breath was coming in short hard bursts now, the pain excruciating, making him wretch, worse than anything he'd ever felt, even the bullet he took once in a Kansas bordello from a man he'd gone to arrest. He could not escape the pain and that was the worst part of it. Then The Gimp, as Gypsy was generally called, wiped the knife blade on his trouser leg and slid his gun into its holster.

Gypsy winked at the dying man before grabbing him under the arms and dragging him to the water's edge where he flipped him face down and shoved his head underwater, and kneeled on the back of his neck, riding him like a weak bronco he was breaking as Charlie Cisco's already waning strength thrashed about, then stopped altogether.

"There you go," Gypsy Flynn said, standing away. "Like that. That's how I like doing it."

He strapped the money belt around his waist and pulled his shirt down over it, then mounted the horse. Taking up the reins of the other horse, he rode back to town and picked up Spade and the woman waiting for him in front of the hotel.

"How'd it go?" Spade asked.

"Just peaches," Gypsy said.

When Spade smiled, it looked like a winter fence blown sideways in his mouth.

The woman asked: "You get the money released?"

"Tried, but that Pinkerton was simply bull-shitting . . . the banker didn't know a damn' thing about any of it."

CHAPTER TWO

It was the woman who spotted them first.

"Riders," she said from the doorway of their cabin.

John Henry Cole had been shoeing the Grulla that was the color of gunsmoke and stopped and looked up and saw them coming through wavering heat that looked like liquid glass rising from the earth. He set the Grulla's foreleg down and said to the woman: "You stay there, in case."

She nodded.

Just inside the door leaning against the wall was a Winchester repeater fully loaded. It was kept in easy reach and she well knew how to use it.

Cole placed his forearms across the Grulla's back and watched the riders come forward. Like the woman in the doorway, he kept a weapon close. Tucked down his belt in the small of his back was a bird's-head Colt Lightning.

The riders slowed as they came up to the cabin and then stopped altogether, their horses huffing and tossing their heads, foam in their mouths from the iron bits.

Cole noticed they rode thoroughbred blooded stock. He took stock of the riders, too—their good riding clothes, the laced-up boots of fine brown leather and brass eyelets, the burl wood stocks of sporting rifles protruding from their saddle boots, the saddles of hand-tooled leather that looked like they'd just come from the store.

The older man who had mustaches the color of cigar ash did the talking: "My name's Wilson. Are you John Henry Cole?"

"I am."

Then Wilson cut his gaze to the woman in the doorway and so did his sons, Bo and Jesse. Cole was ready to turn them out if they said anything about her, but Wilson only said: "Me and my boys, here, have traveled from the Judith Basin. Maybe you heard of it, maybe you haven't. It's of no matter. I am told you hire out."

"Depends," Cole said.

"Depends on what?"

"On what sort of work you're offering."

"I'm needing to find the men who have taken my wife," Wilson said.

"Jesus, Pa," the elder of the two boys said. "Ain't we wasted enough money and time on this?"

"You be quiet, Bo, let me conduct my business," Wilson said.

The other boy simply kept his eyes on the woman standing in the door, her long black hair, the fact she was dressed in a man's checked wool shirt, a plain skirt, beaded moccasins. He knew she was an Indian, but that is all he knew, guessing she was maybe Sioux or Cheyenne being this far north. He had heard they were throat-cutters—the same ones who wiped out Custer.

"I apologize for my son," Wilson said.

"A man reaps what he sows," Cole observed.

"I will pay you a good amount of money to help me get her back," Wilson continued. "Five thousand dollars to be exact."

Cole was silent a moment. "That's a lot of money, Mister Wilson."

"Yes," Wilson said. "No amount of money compares to what my wife is worth to me."

"It's still a lot of money," Cole said.

"These men who have her. They sent me this." Wilson reached into his jacket pocket and, taking out a letter in a brown envelope, leaned to hand it to Cole. "You can read?"

Cole nodded, and took the letter and read it and folded it and placed it back in the envelope and handed it back to Wilson.

"You know this man?" Wilson asked.

"I do."

"Do you think you can locate him before . . . ?"

"So you already paid a ransom and now you're ready to risk paying as much more to find her?"

"Yes," Wilson said.

Cole glanced at the elder boy, the one who'd spoken up. He would be the one to present trouble in a tight fix, he thought. All mouth, maybe a gunfighter, maybe not, but he was strapped with an iron on his hip. Cole could see the bulge of it beneath his coat flap. Same with the other one. But Wilson himself seemed unarmed except for the sporting rifle.

The other one, the shy one staring at Cole's woman, he'd be the one to run. Wilson himself would stand and fight but probably wouldn't be much good at it. Men with plenty of money and smooth hands and fancy clothes who paid other men to do their bidding, well, what did they know about fighting? But Wilson had the look of a grieving man and maybe he was willing to do more than pay a huge sum of money for what was his. Stand up in a fight maybe. Maybe he was even willing to die to get his woman back. He had come a long distance just to offer to hire him.

"If we catch up to these men," Cole said, "it might well get bloody. Lucky Jack's the sort of man who won't run from a fight and won't give up easily what's his."

"She is *not* his."

"Just meant to say, he has her, you don't."

"You know him well, this Lucky Jack?" Wilson said.

"Well enough."

"My sons"—Wilson said with a toss of his head—"would have me do nothing more. They fear that I'm a fool, that this man may have already murdered her just as he did that Pinkerton detective I sent to find her."

"Your boys might be right on that score, Mister Wilson."

"I'll believe it when I find her body."

"Would you have her back, knowing what those men might well have done to her?"

Wilson's face tightened into a grimace as he blinked back tears of either pain or hatred. "She *is* my wife," he said, "and I'll have her back however I find her."

"I'll talk it over with my woman," Cole said. "Rest yourselves, if you like. There is water in the tank for your horses, and I'll have her fix you something to eat."

Wilson nodded. He and his sons dismounted and led their horses to the watering tank while Cole went to the cabin. The woman followed him inside. He spoke to her in her language because it was easier for her, her English still not very good. Cole called her Woman, the name given her by the Crows. She had only been widowed ten years and had lived with her people on the reservation until she had met John Henry Cole who'd hired her to keep his house and cook. But once Cole's son Tom hired on as the town marshal over in Red Pony, Cole and Woman's relationship took a turn, and before either of them realized it they had become the same as man and wife.

"Those men want to pay me to take them and

find the wife of one of them," he said. "How do you feel about that?"

She was slender and half a head shorter than Cole. She was not beautiful in the classic sense, but dark and comely to him with her straight black hair and finely sculpted features that seemed nobler than simple beauty. There was dark mystery in her eyes that he knew he'd never understand completely and he accepted it.

She shook her head. "If you want to go, go," she said.

"I don't want to go . . . but it's a lot of money."

She shrugged. "Why ask me? You will do what you want to do anyway."

"Because . . . ," he said, but had no definitive answer. She was like that. She would never reveal her true emotions, or rarely so, and it complicated their relationship because Cole was not used to such independence in a woman and was still trying to adapt as much to her ways as she was to his. "Will you fix them some food?"

Without answer she set to work preparing cold biscuits and smoked antelope meat, cutting it from a shank.

"We can use the money to fix up things around here, get you a washing machine, a few new dresses, whatever you like," he said.

No answer. She put the pieces of meat with the biscuits in a woven basket and held it out to him.

"A heap of money," he said.

Her gaze was detached, her mouth finely sculpted in a way no human hand could replicate in art. How he enjoyed kissing her in the dark of night, or with the lamp lit, even in the middle of the day. Everything about her aroused him, even her anger and the inscrutable gaze she offered him now. Her limbs were taut, her buttocks firm, her strength surprising. He did not even know her age, and did not care.

"OK," he said. "I'll take them the food and then decide."

She turned back to the shank of meat, rewrapping it in cheesecloth as if he wasn't even there, and carried it out to the smokehouse where she hung it from a metal hook, the interior cool and dry, a spring bubbling up from where two crock jugs were sunken in the earth.

Cole went out with the food, and handed it to the squatting trio of men. "We'll leave in an hour, but I want half the money up front, right now."

Wilson nodded toward his elder boy. "Go and get it from the saddlebag."

Churlishly Bo Wilson stood and went to his father's tall mare and got an envelope from the saddlebag, then returned and handed it to Cole.

"You can count it if you like," Wilson said.

"I will," Cole said, and walked back to the cabin. He counted it and then stacked it on the table. "That's half the money. Find a safe spot for it," he said to Woman.

She barely glanced at it. "I'll pack your things," she said, and went into an off room. He followed her in there and stood watching as she got a large blanket to use for a bedroll and began putting on it a couple of extra shirts, socks, his razor and comb and other things she figured he would need for a journey.

"I'll need my raincoat, too," he said. "I'll get it."

He went out and came back with the rubber slicker. Approaching Woman from behind, he put his arms around her and breathed deeply of her freshly washed hair. It was her custom to go down to the stream that ran north and south along the edge of the property and bathe, and often they would go together and wash each other with a bar of store-bought soap with lavender scent, one of the few luxuries she asked for.

"I love you, I think," he said in English. "Even though you drive me crazy with your mysterious ways."

She did not move but let him hold her close to him, his hands sliding up to her breasts that had their own precise weight that he balanced in his hands. She stood stockstill as he then ran his hands over her.

"I know I don't hardly ever say it, but I'm in love with you, Woman," he said.

He kissed the nape of her neck, having moved her hair aside. She remained as still as a deer in the forest. Under his left hand, now cupping her breast, he felt the beating heart. He turned her and kissed those finely etched lips.

She looked into his eyes without giving away what she was thinking. Sometimes he felt he was taking advantage of her because she would grow very quiet and still like she was now and allow him to do whatever he desired. At other times she became the aggressor, sometimes waking him in the middle of the night, her hand gripping him and tugging him awake before she slid atop him and gently began rocking. He loved seeing her naked in moonlight.

"Go," she said simply.

"I will . . . in a few minutes."

Nearly an hour later John Henry Cole came from the cabin with his bedroll and saddlebags and rifle, the bird's-head Colt now slung in a shoulder holster under his jacket, his worn and stained John B. Stetson settled onto his head, the curled brim shading his eyes and the waning pleasure that was still in them.

Woman stood in the doorway and watched him saddle the Grulla and tie on the bedroll and his slicker and affix the saddlebags and slip the brass-fitted Henry rifle down into the boot, then mount and, without a backward glance at her, ride away with the men.

I don't know that I will ever understand him, she

thought, watching the specter of them growing smaller and smaller. *He comes and he goes as he pleases, and yet he asks me if he should go or not. Men are still like boys no matter how old they are, wanting approval. But him, well, he only asks me these things knowing he is going to do them no matter what I say, so why should I say anything?*

He was not like her dead husband, a scout killed at the Little Big Horn, Walks Slow. Walks Slow was more boisterous, more a man who liked to play jokes on others. But this white man was more serious, quieter, and, maybe, she thought, more dangerous. She smiled a slight and bitter-sweet smile as she watched the shape of him and the other riders fade into the distance, hoping he would return again and force her to yield her body to him. *He is like the wolf that seeks the rabbit and I am the rabbit that does not mind so much being caught.*

CHAPTER THREE

John Henry Cole squatted on his boot heels, gazing across the vast expanse of white and barren land. Waves of heat shimmered from the hard and cracked crust, and beyond in the pale distance was what he knew to be the broken land called Badlands, a wonderful place for men who wanted to lose themselves on purpose. Lawmen called it the Devil's Garden. This much Cole knew and because he'd been there before—not to lose himself, but to find lost men who did not want to be found.

"Yonder beyond this alkali flat and into that broken country is where Gun Town is," he said. "It's where we'll find Lucky Jack and possibly your woman, and maybe where we'll find death, or it will find us."

Wilson stared from under the wide brim of his Montana Peak hat that was so new it didn't even have sweat stains.

"How far?" Wilson said. "Once we cross these alkali flats?"

"Two, three days' ride," Cole said, reaching into his shirt pocket for his pouch of Bull Durham and papers.

"Then we should get started."

"No, not yet," Cole disagreed, funneling a

patch of paper to shake tobacco in. He did this deftly and without thought, a thing he'd done a thousand times before, starting when he was sixteen and working old man Hamm's ranch down on the Niobrara in Nebraska country.

Old man Hamm was a hard boot who had gone up every cow trail ever made out of Texas and into Kansas, New Mexico, and even Montana. He was a top hand until he busted a hip with a bullet from his own gun that discharged accidentally while he was popping mossy horns out of a thicket.

"I'm a god-damn' son-of-a-bitch!" he yelped at the time. He related to Cole, who was then just a greenhorn himself and getting started in the ways of working from horseback: "I never figured to shoot my ownself, but that's what I did and it's the only time I ever shot anybody. Well, I'll pay hell for it. Stormy days'll remind me of how dumb I was."

It was Hamm who taught him to smoke. He also bought Cole, the boy he called Dutch for some reason, his first *bona-fide* whore in the Applejack Saloon in Abilene, Kansas the same night Louisville Lou shot and killed another whore named Jenny Lyons, about which ballads were sung later on.

Hamm and Cole were just up the street at a bordello named the Library, a building of pink, pressed brick operated by Madam Flo Holden

31

who Hamm said had the best-looking whores in the country and he wasn't lying. They had just concluded their business when the shooting began.

Hamm, being a sort of nosy fellow, insisted on going and seeing what the commotion was about. When they entered the Applejack, half the cowpunchers had already dived out of windows and the others were hugging the floorboards. Louisville Lou had shot up the place, including her rival Jenny Lyon, both backbar mirrors, several bottles of Old Tub bourbon, and an ormolu lamp.

Wild Bill Hickok and two deputies disarmed her while she was cursing the name of her dying victim. She was later acquitted by a jury that deemed the shooting a case of self-defense.

Old Hamm died peacefully in his sleep from lung fever. *So many years ago,* Cole thought as he built his cigarette and smoked it.

"Why not cross now?" the churlish elder son Bo asked.

"The horses are already lathered and crossing that wasteland now in the midday heat will only kill them and, if they die, we die. Nobody makes it across on foot."

Cole rose to his full height, the smoke from his cigarette curling upward like wraiths in search of a heavenly home. His was the face of a Westerner, a man who all his adult life had been exposed to hot wind and merciless sun and blistering cold winters, a face deeply tanned under the shade of a creased and now sweat-stained John B. Stetson he'd owned so long he hardly knew he even had it on.

"It don't look that bad," Bo Wilson said. "We ought to keep going if we're going, otherwise let's just turn back."

The older man looked at his son through weary eyes. "I'm not going to tell you again," he said. Then, looking at Cole, he said: "I need to ask you a question of this man, Mister Cole. Do you think he is the sort of man who would . . . take my wife's life?"

"I can't answer that. All I can do is help you find Lucky Jack, and then we'll know."

The older man's body slackened as he sat in the saddle, a pained look on his face, streaks of sweat running down his temples. "Then I'd as soon not wait until night to go after them," he said. "We've got plenty of water in our canteens."

"Not for us and the horses we don't. I'll not run my horse to death," Cole stated. "You are free to go without me, if you want. You didn't hire me to kill us all."

"Shit," the elder son said disgustedly. "It's nothing but a fool's errand as it stands. This fellow here isn't going to do any more for you than that Pinkerton, and probably a lot less."

"I told you to hush your mouth," Wilson said,

but without a great deal of strength or resolve behind it.

Meanwhile the younger boy sat silently on his paint horse. He couldn't have been more than seventeen, eighteen years old, Cole guessed. But the elder one, Bo Wilson, was also too young in Cole's mind to have a mouth on him like he did. If he kept it up, he would one day talk himself into an early grave.

"We'll go and rest in the shade of that adobe until the sun goes down, and then we'll cross," Cole said with finality.

Wilson had wanted to press the chase from the start but had required frequent stops to rest from some painful but unspoken condition he was suffering. It was only after Cole had agreed to take the job that he had begun to notice that something was wrong with the man, pain etched all over his face like it had been cut in by a straight razor.

The sons were young and posed no danger of slowing them down, but the father was another story. The father did not protest too strongly the suggestion that they go and rest in the shade of a lone adobe that sat at the edge of the alkali flats where a line of pines and scrub had petered out as though knowing there was no more water to be had. The adobe was the only structure they'd seen since early morning when they left Cutthroat River where they'd eaten a spare breakfast of scrambled eggs and black Arbuckle's sold by a Dutchman and his wife from a dugout.

Cole mounted his Grulla, and the four of them rode over to the adobe where a top-heavy half-breed woman sat in front of the door on a cane-bottom chair in need of painting. A single bore shotgun rested across her knees. She looked clownish beneath a battered stovepipe hat, one side of it crushed down, the brim half eaten by mice. She eyed the men warily. Her round face was a brown map of disappointed history, her eyes like the beads of a rosary.

A hot dry wind shuffled along the hardpan and spun several dust devils into existence that went spinning out across the flats then died like shot dancers.

"*Señora, algunos alimentos por favor.*"

"Frijoles, tortillas, *poquita cerveza.*"

Cole nodded.

She stood and shuffled inside the mud building with its brown walls that were cracked from dryness and age. The adobe seemed out of place in this north country, and a mystery to anyone who came upon it. Most of the abodes in this country were notched logs chinked with mud and with split shake roofs.

Cole said: "The woman will bring us something to eat. Water your horses and unsaddle them."

There was a rusty metal water tank at the

end of the adobe fed intermittently by a pipe at the bottom of a creaking windmill that turned every so often, some of the blades missing. The water from the pipe would spurt out like blood pumping from a cut artery. They led their horses to drink before uncinching the saddles in the adobe's shade and dropping them on the ground with the horse blankets atop the saddles to air out.

Cole slipped down with his back against the wall and built another cigarette and smoked it in silence while the others either followed suit or sat in the dust.

After a time the woman came with a basket of warm flat bread, a pot of beans, and an *olla* of some sort of home brew and four clay cups. She set these on the ground before the men. They watched as she poured them each a cup of the brownish brew.

"*¿Cuánto, señora, por los alimentos?*" Cole asked.

She held up two fingers.

"What's she want?" Wilson said.

"To be paid . . . two dollars."

Wilson nodded at the elder son. "Pay her, Bo."

The son dug two silver dollars from the front pocket of his jeans and set it down on the basket without bothering to hand it to her. She fisted the money then resumed her post, taking up the shotgun again.

"What's she doing 'way out here?" the younger son Jesse asked, filling one of the tortillas with beans.

"What anyone does," Cole said. "Exist, trying her best to survive one more day. It's all this land will allow."

The other son Bo took a drink of the brew and spat it out, cursing: "Jesus Christ! Tastes like warm horse piss."

"You've drunk horse piss, have you?" Cole said. "Enough to compare?"

The boy glared at him. "I don't like you much," he said.

"Well, your father isn't paying me to be likeable, boy."

"Bo," the older man hissed, "mind your manners."

The four of them ate in the slowly shifting shade, spooned the chili beans into their mouths, washed it down with the beer, and sopped up their plates with the tortillas.

Wilson ate little, his color pale, nearly blood-less. He ate a little bit of the bread dipped in the bean gravy and swallowed a little brew, but that was all.

The others ate in silence as the sun crossed the cloudless sky, dragging time with it. There were only the buzzing of flies around the food to disturb the quiet, the breathing of the men, the hot dry gusts of wind that scattered grit over everything, the swishing of the horses' tails, the old woman's boisterous breathing.

After eating, Cole sat with his back to the cool adobe wall, tipped his hat down over his eyes, and rested. The two sons tried to follow suit but were unaccustomed to sleeping sitting up in a strange place that was hot and desolate and inhospitable, so far from their comfortable quarters and easy life. Back home they had everything a man could want, and when they gave orders, other men did their bidding. But out here they had nothing but themselves and they were taking, not giving, orders from a man they neither knew nor very much trusted. Had it not been for their mother's dying, the elder boy reasoned privately, they wouldn't be here in this far-flung country in pursuit of murderous men and a young and attractive stepmother who, at least as far as Bo was concerned, wasn't worth spit.

In his estimation she was just a trollop that the old man had married less than a year before while on a business trip to Denver. It had been a surprise to both his sons, just as he'd wanted it. Wilson felt he neither needed nor sought their approval, that at the age of sixty-three years old he was his own man.

Bo Wilson found it ludicrous that his father would marry a woman just a few years older than himself, and it would not take all that long to bear out his distrust and assumptions about what she truly was. The younger son Jesse, on the other hand, wasn't displeased that his father had found new happiness and therefore had been more accepting of his new stepmother. In Bo's estimation, his kid brother was naïve and not very smart. And now here they were, trying to get her back. Bo fumed inwardly. Let her go wherever it was those men were taking her. Good riddance. He had been against going after her from the outset, ever since the train's engineer had announced the robbery and her kidnapping on its arrival in Judith. He figured she was getting her due for what had happened between them before.

Adding salt to the wound was the fact that his father had already hired one man to find and return her—a Pinkerton agent. He had paid him $1,000 plus the ransom money of $5,000 that this Lucky Jack fellow had demanded, and gotten nothing in return but word that the Pinkerton man was dead, found floating in the river, cut up like a fish.

Cole dozed in the peaceful shade until the sun came around and touched his boots, and then he stirred and shifted again, and so did the others. Wilson sat with his head down, his eyes closed, his body a brush fire of growing pain that started deep in his nether regions and flared out into his hips and tail bone. The pain had been with him for the past six months but he hadn't admitted it to anyone. He'd thought at first it was just from being pounded in the saddle all those years of riding horseback, having practically been born in the saddle, the way his old daddy used to say. A man gets old, he told himself and it all catches up with him. That's all it was, just getting old, to where he couldn't ride so much as he once could. The pain spoke to him the worst when he and his new wife Lenora made love up in their room in the big house. It would stab him in the lower back and seem to slice him from stem to stern, causing him to catch his breath sometimes and leave his heart hammering in his chest. Once she asked him if something was wrong, and he said it wasn't anything and tried to make light of it. But it kept getting worse, little by little, though there were some days when it hardly affected him at all, but then there were other days when it hurt so bad just to get out of bed. Now the pain was alive inside him, a monster with sharp ravenous teeth and he wished he hadn't run out of those dope pills the doctor he'd gone to see had given him. The doctor had wanted him to see a specialist in New York but he refused to hear of it. "Just give me something to rub the sharp edge off and I'll be all right," he'd said.

"It might be more serious than you think, Wilson," the doctor had warned.

"It's not anything I can't handle, Doc. I'm just

out of that sort of shape, if you know what I mean."

"Well, a young woman like that could certainly do that to a fellow not used to it."

They drank a jigger of whiskey apiece, Wilson washing down one of the dope pills with the bourbon, and then the two of them smoked cigars and talked, trying to remember when the last time they had gone fishing in the Judith River up in Wyoming had been.

These last few weeks in the saddle had begun to take a heavy toll, but Wilson wasn't about to admit to anything, because it would pass as soon as he got Lenora back and things got to be normal again.

The old woman sat, watching the road that led wayfaring wanderers past her place. Not many came, and those who crossed the alkali flats from the opposite direction never came, and those who crossed it from her place she never saw again. She knew the flats were cursed and she called their crossing *el viaje de la muerte*: the journey of death.

She shifted her attention to the memory of a young man, a slight dark-haired boy she'd once loved, a boy murdered too soon by an *Americano* lawman, a *buscadero*, wearing a tin badge who shot her lover in the heart. The boy's blood still stained the flooring of her bedroom, a stain shaped like a misshapen heart. They had buried his body in the cemetery of soldiers and whores and she went to visit him once in a while when her aged body did not betray her.

Now these new men had come no doubt in search of something or someone. She believed that it was a woman they were looking for because two nights previously she had dreamed that men would come and be looking for a woman. She knew that the desire for certain women made men do incomprehensible things. Her Billito was like that. If he had not come to see her that fateful night, then the lawman would not have shot him and he would still be alive. Billito knew the dangers and yet he came because of his desire for her. Bones, she thought. Soon we will all be simply bones, forgotten, turned to powder, as white as those alkali flats and not even a memory, with no one to love us. She watched the older man most carefully, for he seemed like a man with longing eyes, a man starved for the love of a woman. A month ago, or maybe it was two, some other men had come and they had had a woman with them. A pretty woman. The sight of them had caused her finger to rest a little tighter on the triggers of the shotgun. But they had no reason to trouble her, an old crone with little to steal. And certainly she had long ago lost whatever physical charms may have aroused them. She'd always felt, except in the case of her lover, that a woman's beauty was a curse more than a blessing. Especially true on a wild frontier. A woman's beauty attracted men of every kind—the old, the ugly, the profane, and even the married ones. Many pretty girls became victims of their own beauty at the hands of lustful men. No, she was glad that she was now old and wrinkled and unattractive to men. But the man she watched, there in his fine riding clothes and laced-up boots with his ashen face and sooty mustaches, she wouldn't mind so much his being attracted to her. *Ha, I wouldn't mind if he stayed around,* she told herself. A feeling long dormant aroused itself in her like a sleeping cat that awakens and slowly and lazily stretches itself. *Ha, I thought you were too old for such dalliances,* she told herself, reaching for her cup of beer. *Maybe not so old after all, eh?* A smile played at her wrinkled lips as she watched the man.

The younger son teased a scorpion with the blade of his knife, pushing it this way and that without wanting to kill it. For him, trying to track down the men who took his stepmother was a great adventure. He had always been a restless boy, easily bored with his schooling, forever looking out the window and dreaming of far-off places. He wanted to explore the known and unknown world, and now he was getting that chance. The flats looked forbidding, and he knew that the men they were going after were

43

dangerous, for they had robbed the train and kidnapped Lenora and shot the engineer in the foot and the brakeman in the belly. But he was eager to catch up to them, eager to fight, as young men are eager at the thought of first going to war. The pistol on his hip, the weight of it felt fine and true, and he was eager to test his bravery. At his age, he did not know what it was like to die. Death seemed forever far away. Young men thought simply of living not of dying, if they thought at all about such things. They also did not consider what it might be like to lose an arm or a leg, to have a jaw shot off, to be crippled for life. No, young men thinking of combat merely thought of the glory. It was always the other guy who died.

"Stop fooling with that damn' thing and step on it before it stings you," his brother said angrily. He was irritable and hot and restless, and if they were going to do this damned rescue, then do it or else turn back. Privately he hoped the men had killed the woman and that they would find her body and it would dissuade his father from going on, and she would be forgotten. And when the old man's time came, everything would be left to him and Jesse. What right did *she* have to anything? His anger at her had been there from the outset. What right did she have to anything?

After walking about a bit to try and walk off his pain, Mr. Wilson settled with his back to the

44

adobe wall next to John Henry Cole and closed his eyes. He tried not to think of what it would be like to ride several more days yet. The old woman's beer made him sleepy.

Bo pulled his brother aside. "We need to keep trying to get him to turn back. Don't you reckon that they've ruined her, those men who took her? Don't you reckon she'll be a damnable shame to any decent man?"

The younger boy was shedding his boyishness like a snake sheds its skin, and he wasn't certain what his brother meant by "ruining" her. "You mean they would have . . . ?"

"What do you think a bunch of men like that would do to a woman looks the way she does? Don't you think they'd violate her in every way they could? Ain't no man gonna be around a woman looks like her and not do something to her."

Jesse hadn't thought of such things. "I just thought they wouldn't do anything to her because they wanted the money, and if they did anything to her, Pa wouldn't pay them."

"Don't be a nitwit! You willing to die over someone like her, ruined as she probably is now?"

Jesse's face became a mask of concern and doubt, troubled by the images of his stepmother being molested, held down, raped. The mere mention of her violation had stirred a conflicting and troubling image he had had of her ever since that one day, weeks before she was kidnapped. He wasn't supposed to see her. His father and brother had gone to town while he was down with fever and a bad chest cold and confined to his bed. All the while they were gone, he floated in and out of sleep. In his conscious moments he could hear her singing in another part of the house. He'd risen weakly to get a glass of water, but instead was drawn to the sound of her voice and went down the hall.

Her singing came from the adjoining parlor; the door was ajar several inches. He looked in and saw her standing before a full-length mirror completely naked while holding one dress and then another to her. He pulled back quickly as if shot and stood breathing heavily because of his chest cold. He felt odd and weak. He had never seen a grown woman naked in person. Bo had a deck of playing cards with pictures of nudes on the back and that was as close as Jesse had come. But to see a woman in the flesh like he had, especially one so beautiful, turned something in him like a key in a lock. He knew he should creep away, go back to his room. She was his stepmother for heaven's sake. He felt at once embarrassed and aroused. And instead of leaving, he looked again. This time she turned suddenly toward the door, without a dress in front of her, completely exposed.

"Is there something you need, Jesse?" she had said.

He had run down the hall and jumped in his bed, completely frightened about what might happen when she told his father. But no mention was ever made of the incident as far as he knew; his father never came to him about it. It was as if it had never happened. But it *had* happened, and now, as he stood there in the waning sunlight, he thought about those men seeing her naked, about what they'd be doing to her, had already done to her. . . .

Finally the sun flared out beyond the scribble of distant hills and Cole roused himself and said: "Let's go."

They saddled their horses and rode off, the old woman watching them go, crossing herself as she did, lonely once more, and blinking like an ancient turtle.

CHAPTER FOUR

They were four ghosts crossing a ghostly white field under a full moon that had risen and replaced the red sun now sunken below the earth's horizon. The thudding hoofs of their horses were the only sound as they moved, two by two, Cole and Wilson at the head, the brothers behind. The heat of the day having dissipated, the air was cool and Cole's big Grulla loped gracefully under him. The horse, big for a mare, was all muscle and bone and had been as wild as the wind once. But liberty was short-lived for the Grulla. It and some of the other mares had been run into a brush corral by horse hunters, then broken to saddle and bit.

Cole had come by the Grulla by sheer accident, pure circumstance. It had been one of several ridden by bandits that made a career of knocking over banks, sticking their guns in the faces of decent men, and threatening to blow them into Kingdom Come if they did not hand over the money. The banks always handed over the money. Only one man—a boy, really—the son of a banker had stood up to them. And when he did, he was shot in the face for his troubles. The boy lived, but was forever deformed and went about with

48

a silk handkerchief covering his shot-away jaw.

Horse breakers, robbers, wanted men, they all turned out to be the same individuals, all former ranch hands, some even married with kids. Banditry paid better than $30 a month and found and was easier then mending winter fence lines. Cole had been hired to bring them in. The horse breaker's name was Mangrove and he was about as hard-bitten an *hombre* as was likely to be found on the back of a horse or behind a gun. Just like any man trapped with no choice but to surrender or fight, Mangrove chose to fight. It was a bad choice. The others had not been so feisty, or foolish, and Cole had arrested them and put them in leg irons, then loaded them into a barred wagon and hauled them to the courthouse in one of the towns that had been robbed. Mangrove he buried where he fell because there wasn't much point in hauling a corpse. Besides payment and some reward money, Cole got the Grulla, Mangrove's saddle and rifle, an 1877 Winchester that he had traded for the Henry, a lesser rifle to be sure but one he now preferred. Such were his possessions as he rode.

After loping for a time, they slowed their mounts to a walk, and still the white land that lay before them seemed endless in the mercurial light. Then suddenly Bo whipped his horse into a full-out gallop and shot past Cole and Wilson, riding far ahead of them.

"Bo!" Wilson called. "Bo, what the hell are you doing?"

Wilson started to give chase but Cole grabbed his bridle. "Let him go. Why kill your horse, too?"

"But . . ."

"Would you prefer to walk afoot across this barren flat?"

Cole recognized the danger the fool kid had put them all in, but there was nothing he could do about it. Bo Wilson and his horse evaporated in the distance. The other boy continued abreast of Wilson and Cole.

"I don't know what got into him, Pa. He's just been a caution ever since . . ."

"Ever since what?"

Jesse Wilson was reluctant to speak.

"Spit it out, boy!"

"Ever since you brought Lenora home, he's been on a tear. I don't know what he don't like about her, but he don't."

Wilson didn't say anything for the longest time, then he simply nodded, thoughtful, wrapped within himself. He sank down in the pain and disappointment like a man trapped in quicksand with no way out.

They rode on as they had been, trotting and walking their horses, because Cole knew it was still a quite a distance across the flats and they might not reach the other side till dawn. But in another hour they found Bo and his horse. The horse was standing, head down, panting so loud it sounded like a blacksmith's bellows. Its tongue was lolling out, its white eyes big and white as biscuits, frightened and uncertain in death's struggle. Its right foreleg was shattered and dangling, its rider seemingly as helpless as his horse.

The others halted. Wilson dismounted and went to his son and with his hat slapped the boy across the face and cursed him.

"God damn you for ruining that horse!"

The boy pushed back, then knocked his father to the ground.

"Get up! Get up and I'll bust your jaw."

"That's enough!" Cole ordered, dismounting.

The boy turned on him, fists balled. "Why you're just a busted-down squawman," he said. "I doubt you could find Saint Louis with a map and you standing in the middle of it. You're just taking this damn' fool for his money, and I'm sick to death of the whole business."

Wilson rose to one knee. Being knocked flat had sent a roar of pain up through him and now his ghostly face was a mask of torture. "Bo . . . ," he said. "Bo . . ."

The boy turned and delivered a kick to his father's ribs.

"Stop right there!" Cole said. "I'll not warn you again."

The boy turned on Cole, and, when he did, he saw the black muzzle of the bird's-head Colt staring at him, the hammer already thumbed back.

"You damned idiot," Cole said. "You killed your horse and now you aim to kill your father?"

"Go to hell," the boy said.

"Probably someday I will, but not this day, and not before you if you persist."

Cole took a quick step forward, and, as he did, the boy stumbled backward. Cole pulled the trigger and shot the suffering horse, the crack of the gun echoing for miles until swallowed up in the far darkness.

"Help your father onto his horse," Cole said, "or I'll leave you here."

Once Bo Wilson got his father into the saddle again, Cole mounted his own horse. "Let's go," he said to Wilson and the younger son.

"What about me?" Bo Wilson pleaded.

"You walk," Cole said, and heeled his horse forward.

"He can ride on behind me," Jesse offered.

"It's your choice, boy, but know this . . . if your horse fails you under the weight of an extra rider, then you'll both be afoot."

"How far have we yet to go?"

"You'll know when you get there. It's as simple as that."

Jesse looked down at his brother. "Grab hold of Willy's tail, Bo."

"What, you ain't gonna let me ride with you?"

"Can't lessen we lose Willy, too."

"Oh, god damn you!"

They started out, the elder boy holding onto the paint horse's tail, hoping upon hope that the journey was not a long one. But it was. And by the time the moon disappeared and night gave way to dawn, Bo Wilson had fallen behind somewhere. They had reached the far side of the alkali flats, but only the three of them.

Wilson dismounted painfully and handed the reins of his horse to Jesse.

"Go back and get Bo," he said.

The boy took the reins and turned about and rode back to get his brother.

"You're a much more generous man than I would be," Cole said, dismounting and airing out the saddle before building himself a cigarette.

The morning light was as soft and gray as the smoke that drifted from Cole's cigarette. Wilson eased himself onto the ground, resting on one elbow to relieve the pain in his loins. He'd chewed the inside of his cheek raw and tasted blood, but the taste of it was nothing compared to the fire in him. There was grass for the horses to crop, and hopefully soon they would find good water.

"How you holding up?" Cole said.

"It's nothing," Wilson said. "Just a little tired is all."

"What's wrong with you, beside the fact you've got a mean bastard for a son?"

Wilson looked up. "What do you mean?"

"I've seen it on your face ever since we started out. You should have told me you were a sick man before I agreed to hire on."

Wilson looked off, blinking his eyes. "Nothing's wrong with me. I'm just getting old and the saddle seems to get a little harder is all. I once fell from a scaffold, and sometimes I get to aching real bad. Nothing to concern yourself over."

"OK. As you say, it's none of my affair."

Cole smoked while Wilson lay back and closed his eyes. Cole wondered what Woman was doing at that very moment. He imagined her as having risen from the bed and probably baking biscuits and frying a pan of bacon and, he hoped, missing him. He admired her much, and on such a morning as this he told himself he should be waking up in the bed and calling her back from the stove to come and lay down with him, to take and give pleasure with her.

In another hour the two sons rode up, Bo looking defeated and yet defiant when he looked at Cole. His clothes were stained with alkali dust and he looked rather miserable, nearly as much so as his father. He slid out of the saddle and crumbled to the ground.

"Time to move," Cole said, standing up and grinding his smoke underfoot, then tightening the cinch on his saddle. The Grulla stood stockstill as he did so, a tall and proud horse.

"I got to rest," Bo Wilson said.

"You can come or you can stay," Cole said.

"He can take turns riding with me and Jesse," Wilson said.

"It's up to you, Mister Wilson . . . your horses, your money, your wife. Everything is up to you until it's not any more."

"What's that supposed to mean?" the angry Bo said.

"Means what it means. We'll do this your father's way until it stops working out, then we'll do it my way. Those blooded horses of yours don't mean anything to me, and if you want to ruin them, then you will. But comes the time when it gets down to the rub and it's me or you or the men we're after, then we'll play my hand and that will be that."

Wilson stood slowly and pulled himself into the saddle, then kicked a foot free of his left stirrup so Bo could climb up behind him, which he did without a word of appreciation for the offering.

"There's a town not far, such as it is, if it's still there and not blown away or abandoned," Cole said. "Maybe we can find a horse to buy, Bo, that you won't kill if your father is willing to pay for it."

Again they started out. Cole followed a map from memory, recalling a shantytown not far beyond the alkali flats called Forty Rod, knowing as he did that such towns sprang up like weeds, only to die like weeds. He could only hope it still stood.

By the time they reached the town of Forty Rod, the sky had turned an ugly and threatening wood-smoke gray, the clouds bunched and low to the ground blown by a cool wind, and within all that the rumble of thunder sounded like iron balls being rolled across a wood floor.

They looked around as they came into the ramshackle town. Not a building stood that was constructed of more than weathered boards. Some had false fronts as if to disguise the ugliness of the place, as if to give it some semblance of respect, of modernity where there was none. Forty Rod had come into existence after a drunken con artist claimed to have found gold, this after he had filed claims on land he measured out to be forty lots in total, with the idea of selling the lots to would-be business owners who would supply the coming gold miners who would not find gold but as such men knew, once the gold fever got you, you never got fully cured of it. Cole was half surprised it still stood, but it did, populated no doubt by those fevered souls still looking for the mother lode.

The main drag was wide and the town itself just two blocks long with scattered houses here and there beyond the business district that consisted primarily of saloons and cathouses, a Chinese laundry, café, mercantile, and livery. Cole had been through here once before, and it looked as though nothing much had changed but the names on some of the businesses painted in black lettering over door fronts. Cole remembered the most popular place was a hog ranch called Hannah's where the whores were as common-looking as frontier wives too long in the breech. Where it had stood was now billed as a variety theater. Variety theater! *Lord,* he thought, *why would such a place need a theater?*

"Sure don't look like much," Wilson said, gripping the horn of his saddle to keep his seat, his body shot through with pain. Bo at this point was riding behind his brother on the paint.

"I reckon we have seen the elephant," Bo said sarcastically.

"Was a place here that served eats." Cole no sooner spoke than he spotted it, although it was now under a different name than it had been. Instead of Ma's Café it was Sunrise Café. They reined in, dismounted, and tied off.

Yellow light shone through the greasy windows, but through the open door they could smell the cooking odors that set the senses alive with hunger—fried meats and onions, the smell of brewed coffee.

They entered and took up residence at an empty table by the window. A couple was already seated along the opposite wall, a man in a black suit and open paper collar and a woman wearing a feathered hat. They sat across from each other and turned their faces to stare at the foursome for a moment, then resumed eating what was on their plates, their forks scraping the china.

A consumptive-looking fellow in a stained apron came from the kitchen area when he heard the bell above the door tinkle and asked them what they'd be having to eat.

"What's the specialty of the house?" Wilson said.

"Specialty?" the man repeated. When he spoke, he revealed a missing tooth up front in his longish horse face so that it looked like a missing door to an awful house of darkness inside. "Mister, we ain't got no specialty. We got steak and we got potatoes and we got eggs and we got oatmeal. That's what we got. But you come tomorrow and maybe we got some bear meat or deer or antelope haunch iffen the hunters come in with a load in their wagons. And maybe we don't got any eggs iffen Missus Peters don't come with the eggs outen her chicken coop."

"Make it a steak then, and some potatoes, fried up well."

The others ordered the same as famished as they were.

"And coffee all around," Cole said. "You do have coffee, don't you?"

"Enough to drown everybody in the county."

"Just enough for the four of us will do," Cole said, trying to match wit for wit.

The waiter nodded and went to the kitchen muttering something to himself and returned a minute later with cups and a pot of coffee. He set it all on the table and said: "You-all help yourselves while I burn you some meat."

CHAPTER FIVE

When they finished eating, Wilson paid the bill and left a silver dollar as tip. Wilson was pale as the ghostly alkali flats they'd just crossed.

"Maybe we ought to figure on staying the night here and move on in the morning," Cole said.

"Maybe," Wilson agreed.

The waiter returned to fill their cups and take away the dirty dishes.

"There still a hotel in town?" Cole asked.

"Why there is iffen you want to call it that. The Waterloo, just up the street . . . across from the bank, only two brick buildings we got in the whole of Forty Rod."

"Used to be one here called the Westerner," Cole said.

"Burned down two, three years ago. Wasn't nothing but clapboard and went up with a tinderbox. Five people fried to a crisp. Hell of a deal. They decided to build the next one of brick. I reckon they figure brick won't burn quite so easy."

The quartet stood away from the table and walked out into the night. A gentle rain had begun to fall and the drops could be heard pattering on the overhang of the boardwalk and off a metal awning that hung over the mercantile. In a way it sounded like music.

They untied their horses and walked them up the street to the hotel, two stories tall and quite grand for such a place, but a room with a bed was still a room with a bed and better than sleeping on the ground another night. They tied off at the hitch post and went in.

A bespectacled boy behind the desk looked up from a thick book he was reading, *Don Quixote*. Sometimes when he got bored reading it, he used it as a doorstop to let in the outside air on warm, muggy evenings. His eyes were bright and blue behind the lenses of his gold-rim spectacles and magnified twice their normal size.

"Gentlemen," he greeted, dog-earing the page he was on.

"Need some rooms," Wilson said. "Three if you've got 'em."

"Why, you're in luck. There's nobody in the place except myself."

"Good."

"Sign the register, please."

Wilson signed for him and his sons, then handed the pen to Cole who used an old alias he used when a deputy marshal, *Mr. Brown*.

The boy took three skeleton keys from a set of cubbyholes behind him and laid them on the counter.

"Does it matter which is which?" Wilson asked.

"No, not a lick, top of the stairs and take your pick. Rooms in front face the street, of course, but the ones in back overlook an alley. Not as entertaining as watching the street when the drunks come out to fight and the whores to cut each other with razors and the cowboys to shoot off their guns, but this is a week night and not much happens till Friday and Saturday."

"Thank you for that information," Wilson said.

The clerk beamed.

Cole and the sons went outside and retrieved their rifles and saddlebags, then all went up the stairs and selected rooms with Wilson in one and Cole in another and the two sons sharing a room.

Cole said: "I'll put away my things and go see if I can find a horse for sale."

"I'll go with you," Bo said.

"No, you won't."

Both of them knew that sooner or later they would come to blows, or worse.

Cole deposited his saddlebags and Henry, and went out again. By the time he hit the street, the rain had begun in earnest and came down in quarter-size drops that pinged off the metal awnings and ran off the eaves of the over-hangs and boiled in the street. When he had been through here years before, when it was a boomtown because of the silver strikes, he recalled it as a lively if artless sort of shebang.

But now it just looked like a sad old woman dressed in widow's weeds.

Directly across the way was a saloon he remembered distinctly and for a reason, only back then it was called the Lucky Strike, and now it was named Bulldog Ike's as indicated by the faded black lettering above the doors. It was in that place that he had experienced the one fond memory of the town—a pretty prostitute named Nell Blue. If he'd been asked at the time, he might have told the inquisitor that he was almost in love with Nell.

Most men would tell you they'd never marry a prostitute, but most men would be lying. Women of any nature and profession were hard to come by in such raw frontier places and Nell had half the men in town in love with her and the other half in lust with her, himself guilty on both counts. He and Nell had only spent one night together, but what a night it was. Funny, he hadn't thought about her for years, until now. There had been plenty of women in between, even a wife, as well as the mother of his second and surviving son Tom. But a man's first real love stays with him throughout the years.

Curiosity got the better of him and he dashed across the street, trying to outrun the large heavy raindrops but without success. He rattled one of the double doors open and entered, feeling both odd and a sense of anticipation thinking there wasn't any way he'd find her still here—hoping that he would and hoping that he wouldn't.

A barrel-chested man with waxed mustaches stood behind the bar, reading an article in a three-week-old issue of *Harper's Weekly* about former pitcher for the Cincinnati Red Stockings Asa Brainarrd who died of pneumonia at the age of forty-seven. The paper was spread out like giant butterfly wings on the oak. He was just to the part about how Asa's old teammates were to wear black armbands when they took the field next against the Baltimore Canaries. The man didn't even bother to look up when Cole entered, so engrossed was he in the story.

The only other occupant in the narrow little place was a character who might have walked right out of the Old Testament, what with his long tangle of beard and rough-looking clothes. His thick eyebrows were hoary horns that arched away from his forehead and lent fierceness to his visage. All he needed was a leather cinch and to be eating locusts and honey.

Cole stepped to the bar.

"What'll it be, bub?" the bartender, aware of him now, asked while he put down a gleaming shot glass.

"Something in that," Cole said. "Kentucky bourbon, if you've got it."

The bartender reached on the top shelf of the

backbar, took down a bottle of Old Tub, and filled the glass.

"Best I carry," he said. "Name's Bulldog Ike."

Cole knocked back the drink and set the glass down, circled a finger over it, and Bulldog Ike refilled it. Cole said: "Damn' fine liquor."

Bulldog Ike smiled like a proud father. "Appreciate a man who appreciates a good glass, this one's on the house."

"Thankee kindly."

Cole watched while Bulldog Ike poured himself a shot of Old Tub, then corked the bottle and set it back on the shelf. "Cheers, mate," he said, lifting his glass for Cole to clink with his own. They both tossed them back.

"I was curious if you ever heard of a gal who used to ply her trade out of here sometime back when it was under a different ownership . . . Nell Blue?"

"She roll you and you're looking for revenge?"

"No, nothing like that. I knew her and we were friends of a sort."

"Just about all the whores left when there proved to be no gold. Sorry, bub, never heard of her, but if you was to find her, you can tell her Bulldog Ike is hiring. It's easier to find a turtle's pecker than a good whore in this town. Oh, we got a few all right, but they're mostly stove-up with bad backs and hips and no teeth. Like fornicating with a knothole."

"Yeah, I'll make sure, if I encounter any beauties, to send them by," Cole said facetiously. He turned to go and the old man in the corner yelped: "I knew Nell Blue, by gar if I didn't. Right fine woman, too. She warn't just any ol' whore. She nursed the sick when the influenza come through here and other such."

Cole went over to the old Peckr's table.

"You know where she might have gone?"

"Yes, sir, for the price of a drink I can tell you exactly where you can find her?"

Cole paused, thinking it over. Would he really want to start something up again with Nell? Was it just idle curiosity, or more than that? Or was it, as he told himself, that there are certain women a man just never can forget no matter how many years pass and how many other women he's come to know?

"Sure," Cole said, and turned toward the barkeep and told him to bring the old boy a shot and a beer, then dropped a silver dollar on the table. "And whatever else you can buy for that."

What teeth the old boy possessed looked like rotted shoe-peg corn left over from a gleaning. His sagging loose lips rode the crest of purple gums, his mouth squashing the words when he talked. The barkeep brought over a shot and a beer and set it before him, shaking his head as he took up the Liberty dollar.

"I get change from that!" the old man yelped again, followed by a squawking laugh, then downed the shot like he was trying to put out a fire in the back of his throat.

"OK," Cole said. "Where can I find her?"

"Cemetery," the old man said, quaffing some of the beer and licking foam from his lips. "Been there ten or so years, as I recollect. Boys in town got together a collection to buy her a tombstone since so many had fond recollections of her. Easy enough to find, hers is one of the few what *have* a headstone with an angel atop. She was an angel, too, even if one that was fallen."

"How'd she die?" Cole asked with a feeling of deep disappointment.

The old man's face twitched. "A fellow shot and killed her. A married fellow, he was, too. Killed her 'cause he was jealous of her with other men. Claimed he was in love with her and didn't want no other man to have her. Shot her right there." He pointed a gnarled finger to a spot where a dark shape stained the floorboards. "Shot her five or six times . . . wanted to make sure she was dead. I was sitting right where I am now, right where I always sit. Back when I had plenty of money in my poke. It was the god-damnedest thing to see them bullets punching the life out of her. Jesus, but the blood." He drank down the rest of his beer and shouted: "Hey, you fat bastard, bring me another!"

"You keep talking like that I'll throw you out into the street, you bum."

"Bum! I ain't no god-damn' bum! Why, hell, I was richer'n any man in this bunghole of a town."

"Maybe once, but Moses, you've not had so much as lint in your filthy pockets all the time I've known you."

They went back and forth like that. Cole suspected it was as much out of boredom as out of animus. "What happened to the man who shot her?" he asked.

Moses blinked as if fighting tears, his old mouth sagging as he said: "They was gonna hang him, but his missus pleaded for his life, said she'd be left a widow and her kids orphans. So a vote was taken and they let him go, but not before Hinkey beat him half to death with a board. Hinkey was her pimp and it was a great loss of income he suffered when Nell passed. So the boys said as long as Hinkey didn't beat him to death, he could have at him for a time. Beat that poor devil all up and down Main Street till he couldn't stand no more . . . bruises from head to toe. Ha! Served him right. Was up to me, I'd have shot off his nuts, and then hanged him." He slapped the table with the flat of his hand so hard it sounded like a pistol shot and said with a cackle: "And you know that son-of-a-bitch turned into a preacher for a time, repenting and telling others to do the same, and for a time we all thought maybe that pimp had beat God into him, but it warn't so. He up and absconded with yet another man's wife what come and prayed in his church, and he's been in the wind ever since. And that poor wife of his who begged for his life, well, she was left to raise them young 'uns by herself after all and moved back to Ohio where they was from originally. The frontier does funny things to folks."

Bulldog Ike set the beer down and said: "Why would you listen to an old fool like him?"

"It's the gol-danged truth, ever' word of it!" Moses said.

"Yes, and I'm the Queen of Sheba," Bulldog Ike said.

"Well, maybe you are, you prissified dandy."

Bulldog Ike stalked off.

"What was that fellow's name, the preacher?" said Cole.

"Why . . . let me think . . . Garden, was it? No wait, something Frenchy sounding . . . *Gardiner,* that was it. Had a funny first name, too. . . ." Moses scratched around in the nest of his beard until the name came to him. "Jules . . . Jules Gardiner. Think he went on up to Gun Town, him and that other fellow's wife. Gun Town. Ha! Perfect place for such devils as him. He might be planted by now if he continued fooling with other men's wives, though I doubt there is many honest women in Gun Town, what with all the trash hangs out up there. Scurrilous vermin, thieves, and murderers."

Cole nearly said that was where he was headed with the Wilsons, but refrained. "Enjoy your drinks," he said instead, and went out, troubled still by the news of Nell's death. She may have been a bride of the multitudes but she had been special to him and she sure as hell didn't deserve being shot to death.

He kept to the covered boardwalk to avoid the rain until he was forced to cross over to a livery he had espied on the way in. He stepped out into the muddy street and entered the livery's horse barn with its sweet scent of hay and horse.

He heard, rather than saw, a human snoring among the horses stamping in their stalls. He followed the sound to an empty stall and saw a small thin boy with corn-yellow hair, lying on his side, knees drawn up, and using his hands for a pillow, sleeping peacefully as a man in a featherbed.

Cole tapped him on the soles of his worn boots until the boy sat up and blinked his eyes against the yellow glow of a nearly burned-down flame inside a bull's-eye lantern.

"What you want?"

"What you got?"

"Huh?"

"Horses," Cole said. "I reckon you sell horses, don't you?"

"Yeah, got one or two I might sell you."

The boy reached and turned up the wick so that the area around them spread with weak light as he stood without bothering to brush the straw from his backside or shirt or hair.

"Let me see 'em."

The boy went to a stall where a mare stood with her head hanging out, a star on her face but her eyes not very bright

"Got Spooky," the boy said. "Could let her go for eighty dollars and toss in a McClellan saddle."

Cole took the lantern and held it closer for examination. What he saw was a one-eyed horse with a swayed back and sickly. "Why that horse wouldn't make it ten miles up the road before she'd drop dead. You got anything that's more than half alive?"

He handed back the lantern as the boy sighed with disapproval of Cole's assessment of Spooky.

"Got another here in the back I might could let go, but he'll cost you more. Name is Vic and he used to belong to General Custer himself."

Cole followed, knowing the story was made up. Everybody who had a horse for sale these days had some sort of fantastical story to tell in order to jack up the price.

The boy held up the lantern to show a wide-eyed buttermilk gelding that bared its teeth and snorted its displeasure, tossing its head so furiously it banged against the stall wall; the pain and surprise caused the horse to lash out with a rear kick that hammered on the boards.

"What ya think?" the boy said, light flaring off his bony features. His shirt was nearly ragged and his coveralls were held up by one strap. He was barefooted and probably had scurvy.

"Not much," Cole said.

"Well, it's what I got for sale. I'd take seventy-five only because he's a bit me twice and I hate the sucker."

When Cole came near, the buttermilk reared its head, its eyes rolling white, its nostrils flaring. It would serve Bo Wilson right to be stuck with such a cantankerous beast.

"He's rank as a mean drunk," Cole said thoughtfully. "I bet the general had a time with him."

"Shit, yeah!"

"It's a joke, kid. Custer wouldn't shoot that horse and eat him, even if he was starving to death."

"Make me an offer. I got to get rid of him."

"Let me think on it."

"Hell," the boy said, disappointed. "You don't happen to have a bottle on you, do you? I could use a nip."

"How old are you?"

"Fifteen, well, almost fifteen."

"You work for the man who owns this place?"

"I do for sure, it's my pap. But he's all the time drunk and laying about . . . mostly ma and me keep things together. Sure could use a nip, rainy night such as this, help warm my bones."

They could hear the rain hammering off the metal roof above their heads, hear it running off the eaves, and splashing into puddles as they reached the entrance.

"Least it ain't snow," the boy said, looking out as they stood in the open entrance. "You don't have to shovel rain." His snigger at his own wit sounded like saw blades scraping together.

"I'll let you know," Cole said again, and ducked back out, hat low over his face to help ward off the rain.

He hurried up the street, trying to avoid getting soaked through. He was the only one out, it seemed, and his boot heels knocked over the loose fitting boards of the sidewalk.

He reached the hotel and went directly to Wilson's room and rapped with his knuckles.

The younger brother Jesse answered the door and allowed Cole to enter. Wilson lay upon the bed, looking stricken, his face bloodless, sweated, twisted in pain. He had his boots off and lay fully dressed with his socks on. Bo Wilson stood at the window, looking out at the rain.

"How you making it, Mister Wilson?" Cole said.

"I think I need to see a doctor," he said in a near whisper.

"Hell, I doubt there is even such a thing as a doctor in this dung heap," Bo said bitterly as he turned his head toward the room.

Wilson raised his watery eyes, then lowered them again.

"I'll go see about a doctor," Cole said.

He went down to the lobby. The bespectacled clerk had given up reading *Don Quixote*. He was painfully shy and given to talking to himself. He looked up as Cole approached. "I need a doctor for Mister Wilson upstairs. There one in town?"

"Well, sorta."

"Yes or no?"

"Got one what treats more animals than humans, but nobody's certain he ever went to medical school and he's a bit tetched in the head."

"Where can I find him?"

"Out the door, down the end of the block, and up the outside stairs of the Blue Star is where he keeps an office, or you might just see him walking down the center of the street, carrying a parasol or some such . . . raving to himself."

Cole found the place and knocked on the door, waited, then knocked again, the rain spilling off the brim of his hat. Finally the door opened and there stood a man in a tattered and stained wedding dress with a barrister's powdered wig upon his head. He was goggle-eyed and had a large nose spidered with tiny red veins. He had a weak chin and was gap-toothed.

"Yes, how might I assist you, sir?"

The wig was askew. The sight of him nearly took Cole's breath away. He shook off the shock and said: "I'm told you're a doctor . . . of sorts."

"Yes, yes, I'm a doctor. I doctor anything that lives and breathes, but the dead I do not dally with. Do no harm, yes, do no harm, do you know where that comes from?"

Cole said: "No, and I don't much give a damn. I have a man that needs medical attention. Are you the only medico in this town?"

"Comes from the Hippocratic oath is where that comes from," the man said, ignoring Cole's question. "First, do no harm." He giggled like a flummoxed girl. "Let me go and get my bag of potions and pills, my cure-alls."

The dress-wearing medico followed Cole to the hotel. Cole took care to stay one step ahead of him in case anyone saw them.

Soon as they entered the room, Bo Wilson said: "What the hell is this?"

Jesse was kneeling by his father, doing the best to comfort him.

"Step aside and let the doctor have a look at your father," Cole said to Jesse.

"That maniac isn't touching my pa," Bo insisted.

"Then you tell me who is?" Cole asked.

"Here, here gentlemen. Let's get on with it, the care of this poor man."

And it was as if the medico had been transformed from a laughingstock to a serious practitioner of the medical arts, a man in control. "I'm Doctor Pursewater," the medico said to Wilson as he pulled up a chair to the bed. "Can you tell me what ails you, where does it hurt?"

Wilson labored to get out words as he cringed and gritted his teeth against the waves of pain that burst inside him like heat lightning.

After getting Wilson's sons to help undress him, the doctor checked Wilson's eyes, then depressed his tongue, looked into his throat, palpitated his lungs, and bent his ear to the man's chest before standing up. "Just point to where the pain is the worst, if you would, sir."

"Right here," Wilson whispered, touching his lower region. "In my groin."

"How bad is your pain?"

Wilson looked up like a dog that had been recently whipped. " 'Bout as bad as anything I ever dealt with. . . ."

Pursewater pressed the lower abdomen, and Wilson recoiled as if he'd been shot. Pursewater said: "I need you to turn over. You ever been examined back here by a doctor?"

Wilson nodded.

"Well, then you know what to expect."

The others looked on as the dress-wearing healer made his final examination using a forefinger. They saw Wilson grit his teeth, the beads of sweat dripping from his face.

"OK, you can turn back over now," Pursewater said, and helped his patient onto his back again.

The medico shook his head and reached into his worn leather bag with its broken brass clasp and took out a small brown bottle, stoppered by a cork.

"Laudanum," he said, twisting out the cork and putting it to Wilson's lips. "Take you a good tug of it. It will rub the edge right off that pain and you'll start to feel relief in a short time." Turning to the others, he announced: "This man cannot ride or travel anywhere for at least several days, if at all."

"What's wrong with him?" Jesse said.

The medico adjusted his wig slightly and said: "It most likely is cancer of the ass, to put it bluntly." It was the same diagnosis as Wilson had gotten from the other doctor, the one with degrees hanging on his office wall, and though the other one hadn't been so crude in his use of language, Wilson knew it meant the same thing.

"Can't you fix him?" Bo Wilson said.

"I could cut him open and scrape out as much as I could find, but I doubt it would do much good if cancer is what it is, and I'd only add to his misery."

Pursewater corked the bottle and set it on the spindle-legged bedside stand.

"Make sure he gets a dose of that whenever he starts to complain."

"How long's he got?" Bo asked.

Pursewater looked at the churlish boy: "He will live as long as he is meant to live and not one day longer . . . just like the rest of us. It was writ in the stars at the beginning of time, and so it shall be. No bullet can kill us if its not meant to be, no cancer nor drowning in nameless rivers, or being struck by lightning. God has arranged everything for us so that we shall not have need to worry as to our number of days. Worry won't change a single hair on your head."

"I suppose you're a preacher, too," Bo said sarcastically.

"Perhaps," said Pursewater, "but judge ye not so that ye won't be judged."

Bo turned away and gazed out the window.

Wilson rallied briefly, turning his face to the others until his gaze came to rest on Cole.

"Come closer, please, so I can talk to you."

CHAPTER SIX

Wilson's nearly colorless eyes turned toward John Henry Cole. "Nothing's changed," he said in a cracking voice. "I paid you to get her back and that's what I want."

"Yes, I can understand that," Cole said. "But wouldn't you rather wait till you get better and are up to riding. We can rent a hack, if need be, and you can ride in that. Pad the seat with blankets and pillows."

Wilson shook his head. "No, I can't wait. The longer it takes, the more likely they are to kill her . . . or worse. I can't imagine what she's going through as it is."

Cole said: "OK, then I'll go on. I'll wire you any news I have . . . either way, good or bad."

Wilson nodded. "Take Bo with you."

"Your boys ought to stay with you," Cole replied, privately wanting nothing to do with the quick-tempered son.

"Jess will stay with me, take Bo."

Now Bo spoke up from where he leaned against the wall, its faded wallpaper of bland roses water-stained in places and sloughing off the plaster like dead skin in other places. "I'm going with you. I need to protect my father's interests."

"What's that supposed to mean?"

79

"It means he's paid you a hell of a lot of money and maybe you'll find the woman or maybe you'll just keep on going. Or just maybe, Lucky Jack will kill you like he did that Pinkerton."

Cole leveled his gaze at Bo Wilson. He was big and strapping, in his early twenties, but in Cole's estimation he was just a damned fool looking for any kind of trouble. "I don't need him," Cole said to Wilson. "I can probably find her quicker if I'm not riding with a horse-killer."

Bo stepped a foot closer to Cole who held up the flat of his hand. "Don't do anything we'll both regret, boy."

It froze the elder son in his tracks.

"I trust you wholeheartedly, Mister Cole," Wilson said. "But I'd like Bo to go along because you just might need his help. I sent one man alone to find her and he ended up dead. I don't want that to happen again. Take him, please."

Cole could see lingering death in Wilson's eyes, watching as if a wild beast were hunkered down in the shadows waiting for the kill. Maybe sooner than the crazed medico had predicted, maybe later, but there it was, the twin candle flames in Wilson's eyes burning down slowly, inexorably. He nodded at last. "Then we'll be going soon as the horses have a good rest, some grain."

Wilson nodded, murmured: "Thank you. . . ." Then he closed his eyes and relaxed into an easy sleep from the laudanum the medico had given him, the sensation of peace coming over him like a night fog.

Cole and Bo Wilson took their horses to the yellow-haired kid at the livery to be grained and watered.

The kid asked: "Ain't you gonna buy my horse?"

"No need, now," Cole said.

Then the two sat out front of the hardware store on a pair of wood chairs, watching it rain. Cole smoked and Bo Wilson fidgeted in pent-up silence.

The rain fell steadily, turning the street into a quagmire that no man dared cross for fear of losing his boots. The drunks came and went from Bulldog Ike's, and one or two stumbled and fell face down into the street and came up, struggling and wiping the mud from themselves.

"What the hell do you think is wrong with that man?" Bo asked, staring between his boots.

"What man?"

"That damn' fool in the wedding dress and powdered wig."

"It's a little like the old lady who kissed the cow said . . . everybody to his own taste."

"Shit, that don't even make sense, what you just said."

"Doesn't have to make sense, boy . . . not much in this world does any more."

"I take offense at the word *boy*."

"You take offense pretty much at everything, I've noticed." Cole began fixing himself another smoke.

"I got a right."

" 'Course you do. But a word of advice. Someday your taking offense so easy is going to get you killed."

"Yeah, well, I reckon if it does, it does. I ain't about to change my ways for no man."

Cole finished rolling his shuck, licked the edge of the paper, and twisted the ends before striking a match he took from his right-hand pocket and raking it across his spur, then cupping the flame with his hands. He drew in a lungful of smoke, then breathed it through his nostrils and watched as the smoke drifted into the sodden air.

"How long you planning on us sitting here?" Bo asked.

"Long enough so our mounts can catch a decent blow, maybe another half hour."

"Well, shit, I reckon I'll walk to that bar and get me a drink of something rather than just setting here doing nothing."

"Suit yourself."

Cole watched the man-child rise from his chair and step out into the rain. He watched him slog through the mud, the mud sticking to his boots until he reached the far side where he scraped it off on the edge of the boardwalk, before entering the saloon. It felt lonesome of a sudden, sitting there alone in the rain in this particular town, having learned the fate of Nell Blue and he being so far away from Woman when he ought to be back there with her and not on some fool's mission to get a woman back from Lucky Jack who'd probably killed her already or sold her into whoredom. He recalled the time Lucky Jack shot four men in less than three seconds in a town not dissimilar to this one—one that was in the Nations back when they were both working as deputy marshals for Judge Parker's court. He'd been waiting out front with the horses, his and Lucky Jack's, while Lucky went inside, looking for the fellows they were after. Neither had figured they'd be inside that saloon. Cole had heard the gunfire. It had sounded like a string of firecrackers, all going off almost as one. By the time Cole had entered the saloon, pistol in hand, cocked and ready to fire, there hadn't been anything but gunsmoke and corpses, except for Lucky Jack.

Lucky Jack had stood at the bar, a pistol in each hand with smoke curling from the muzzles and the Elton brothers dead on the floor, their ma unlucky enough to have had two sets of twins as her only children that were now no more. One of them had gotten off a round that had cracked Lucky Jack's shoulder bone and another had put a hole clean through his new Stetson. It lay on the floor near one of the brothers. Blood had soaked Lucky Jack's left sleeve and was dripping off his fingers and the gun in his hand. He hadn't seemed at all fazed. The fact was that Lucky Jack nearly shot Cole, coming through the door before he had shouted: "Hold up, partner!" Then Lucky Jack had lowered his pistols even though he still had that glazed, killing look in his eyes.

"Well, we found the bastards," had been all Lucky Jack had said a moment later while exploring the hole in his new hat and flexing his wounded shoulder. He had ordered a whiskey for each of them, and, when it was poured, had calmly put the hat on his head, held up his glass, saying—"Cheers."—and had promptly passed out cold.

Later, when he had awakened under the force of smelling salts held to his nose by a doctor—this one not in a dress but in a wrinkled black coat—Lucky Jack had looked about and said: "What the hell happened?"

"You were shot," Cole had told him, and helped Lucky sit up, his back against the bar's facing.

Lucky Jack had looked at the blood leaking from him and said: "Feels like I got hit with a piece of hickory." Then he had passed out again.

It was the damnedest display of bravado Cole had ever witnessed, and he knew now that once Lucky Jack had gone over to the dark side of life, he had became a force of Nature, a first-class killer and no one to fool with. Facing him down would be akin to reaching your hand into a box of rattlers and praying you didn't get bit but knowing you would, and terribly so. And now he and this fiery kid were going to ride right into Lucky Jack's camp and try and retrieve a woman he'd stolen. Cole shook his head as though he'd just lost his last dollar betting on a three-legged horse in a stakes race.

When another half hour had passed and the kid wasn't back yet, Cole stood and crossed the street, the rain not having let up a drop, his boots sinking down past his ankles, and entered the saloon. He didn't see the kid.

"Where'd that tall kid go that come in here half an hour ago?" Cole said to Bulldog Ike.

It was the old reprobate who spoke first.

"Went out back with Dora to get his pizzle oiled," Moses said with a cackle. "He's liable to think he's met Jesus, time Dora gets done with him."

Bulldog Ike nodded toward a hall that led toward the back. "Where the dirty business is conducted," he said.

Cole ordered a beer, figuring if the kid hadn't come out by the time he finished it, he'd go back and get him. He had quit drinking for a time, but now he found, he could drink in moderation and not be compelled to continue until he was blind drunk. He was just about on his last swallow when Bo Wilson appeared still buckling up his front with a chubby, apple-cheeked gal who looked old enough to be his mama following.

"How's about buying Dora a drink, sonny," she said, "you know, in appreciation for the good time I showed you."

Bo started to say something, probably something insulting, but Cole intervened. "Let's go," he said.

For the first time Bo Wilson looked abashed over something, said nothing, and followed Cole out and down to the livery where they got their horses. They mounted up and rode out of town like a pair of deuces looking to land work.

CHAPTER SEVEN

The place everyone called Gun Town was a rambling, shambling collection of wooden structures sprung up from the earth to support the habitués of a lower order of men and women—a veritable refugee camp of gun artists, cardsharps, drifting saddle tramps, bank robbers, ex-Confederates, and a few more or less honest types who owned the more or less honest businesses that served any population. Gun Town fell mostly under the control, if control it could be called, of various toughs who, like snarling wolves, yipped and snapped at each other's heels and sometimes drew blood and sometimes had it drawn. The only semblance of law was a down-on-his-heels and long-in-the-tooth lawman and long-standing friend of Lucky Jack's named Bill Hammer. Why there was any law at all was a mystery, except to the consortium of business owners who demanded that someone be given the power to arrest drunks and minor troublemakers in order to hold down the costs of doing business—such as when the aforementioned busted up chairs and started fistfights or attempted to rob one of their own. Criminality was allowed everywhere but within the town limits was the adopted philosophy.

And to that end, Lucky Jack had summoned old Bill Hammer out of sentiment, hearing that his old pal was swamping out saloons in Bozeman. Bill Hammer had long ago swallowed any pride he once had. Among the local gangs, Lucky Jack's was the most vicious. This former deputy U.S. marshal lived above Karl's Liberty Palace Saloon, and when not off somewhere knocking over banks or trains, he observed his kingdom from a specially constructed perch that jutted out from the upper floor overlooking the main drag where he could keep an eye on the comings and goings of strangers. Within was a double apartment where he conducted business, gave orders, and planned his next crime. It was here he had planned his latest scheme and from whence he and his crew went to rob the Judith Basin flyer knowing already who would be on it.

While John Henry Cole and the hot-tempered Bo Wilson were still several days out, Lucky sat on his specially built verandah, the evening misty and cool, smoking a cigar while Miss High and Mighty, as he'd come to call her, lingered inside, stretched across the bed.

My little empire, he thought. *Now tell me where an honest man can do this well for himself?* He smiled around the cheroot.

Lucky Jack was a big man at well over six foot tall, and wide through the chest and shoulders.

But for the welt of bluish scar that ran from ear to jawbone, his was a countenance of near perfection with its crisp green eyes intense beneath a wide brow, his face solid as stone. Some said it was dangerous even to look at him. Every miscreant in the Nations feared the name Lucky Jack built from his reputation as a shoot-first, ask-questions-later deputy U.S. marshal. The bones of those who had taken him lightly were presently fertilizing the Oklahoma soil, like the four brothers in that tavern that day in Ardmore.

Again he smiled around the stogie, heard her in there, coughing from the whiskey vapors. Miss High and Mighty. He saw Gypsy Flynn, who everyone called The Gimp, come limping across the street. Gypsy was a fooler: he looked weak and incapable on account of his limp from having chopped off his own toes with an axe while he was in Yuma prison since it was a way to get sent to the infirmary where he killed an orderly and made his escape. Hardly anybody could believe such a story until Gypsy showed them his foot, four of his five toes but nubbins. The littlest toe had survived and looked like a pink worm dangling at the edge of his foot. But it was Gypsy who had put the knife in that Pinkerton and a whole lot of others, too. Did it without caution or regret. Did it almost gleefully.

Gypsy described in great detail how he'd knifed

the Pinkerton before drowning him. Truth be told, it caused Lucky's skin to crawl just listening to him. It was Gypsy who also said the reason he'd done it to the Pinkerton was because there wasn't no money, that the Pinkerton confessed as much.

"It's the reason I put the blade in him, Lucky," Gypsy said. Afterward Lucky had the woman write her husband a letter describing the events of the Pinkerton's death and as a warning that next time Wilson had better bring the money himself if he didn't want his wife to suffer the same fate. What Gypsy didn't include in his murderous tale to his boss was how he'd stashed the money belt beneath the floorboards of the miner's shack in which he lived. Nor did Gypsy speak of further plans he also had—to take the next $5,000 from Wilson and then finish Lucky the same way he had finished the detective.

"Make sure you write in there about him coming alone," Lucky Jack had instructed Lenora.

"He won't," she had said.

"Sure he will. He loves you, don't he?"

"I doubt ten thousand dollars' worth," she had said.

"Then put in there that, if he don't come, I'm going to sell you to a chink whorehouse."

She glared at Lucky when he said that. "You wouldn't."

"You think I wouldn't?"

"Damn you!"

She had tried to stab him with the nib of the pen with which she was writing the letter. He had grabbed her wrist and stayed the hand. "I like you when you're fiery."

"I hate you!" she had screamed.

"You didn't always."

"Always was a long time ago, Lucky."

He had offered her that toothy smile that had won the hearts of many women, and won hers as well, though theirs had always been a rocky relationship.

"We got to milk your husband for all we can get. Got to make it look good."

Her eyes had been smoky and smoldering at the same time. "I don't know why I ever let you talk me into this," she had said.

"Because you know you'll do anything I tell you. Now finish the damn' letter."

"I won't!"

He had dragged her to the bed, ripped off the dressing gown she was wearing, his eyes taking in her beautiful nakedness, a sight he didn't think he'd ever get tired of seeing. But then again, there were plenty of other beautiful women in the world, weren't there? And he had reminded her of this whenever she got balky. She had slapped him hard across the face and he had slapped her back, his blow splitting the corner of her lip drawing blood.

"Damn you!" she had cried.

"You like it, don't you? That's the thing about me and you, Miss High and Mighty. I know what you like and you know what I like, and we give each other what we like. Nobody understands us but us."

She had touched the blood on her lip with the tips of her fingers, stared at it a moment, then had licked her fingers and smashed her mouth to his and bit his lip, also drawing blood. He had thrown her onto the bed, cursing her as he did, as he had stripped out of his clothes. As he had fallen upon her and forced her to yield herself to him and kept forcing her until she had cried out a sound that, if heard, could not be discerned between pleasure or pain.

Afterward she had finished the letter and signed it, kissing it so that a drop of her blood stained it, then sprinkled some water from a pitcher in the room on it so that the water looked like tear drops.

"Satisfied?" she had said, holding it up for him to read.

"Yeah, send it," he had said. "Then let's go down to the bar tonight and have a drink, or maybe two."

She had thought about that poor fool that had married her. Lucky Jack had sent her forth on a mission—meet and marry a rich man. And that is what she had done. But later she wasn't as sure as she had been about it all. She had told herself she'd done a lot of low things in her life, but maybe this was the lowest of them all.

Wilson had been good to her, kind and loving and chivalrous, had bucked his own sons on account of her. He had bought her fancy clothes through the mail order, some from Paris, France, and perfumes, and the latest in hat wear. And though she did not love him, could not love him, still she had felt sorry for him. Men were so easily fooled, so easily betrayed, especially if the betrayal came from a beautiful young woman who spoke and carried herself well. And yes, she'd had to be intimate with him, but she had the capacity to put her mind somewhere else whenever experiencing anything unpleasant. The darkness had helped, too.

She thought of her life as two separate epochs—before Lucky Jack and after Lucky Jack. Before, nothing much counted. But after she'd met him, everything had intensified and he was more than her equal in every way and for that reason she was unable to resist him and mourned when she was separated from him and rejoiced when reunited. He was her one great weakness. There was no getting around that. She couldn't have explained it even to her best friend, though she had none—for to whom does a woman turn for confidences who is herself somewhere between a lady and a harlot?

Well, she had slipped on a dress of red satin—

blood-red—and laced-up, black, high-button shoes, then swept and pinned up her deep brunette hair with ivory combs in order to be ready to go down to the saloon for a drink or two, thinking as she went, maybe Wilson would be smart enough to see through the ruse and not come at all. If he didn't come, perhaps that would be the end of it. She was more than afraid that the poor man would be murdered either by Lucky, or worse by that weasel, Gypsy Flynn. She didn't want Wilson's blood on her hands. She could only hope.

CHAPTER EIGHT

For two days more they rode, John Henry Cole and Wilson's firebrand son, mostly in silence having little in common to talk about. But every now and then, just for something to distract his boredom, Bo Wilson would ask a question or make a comment.

"How the hell does anyone find their way through this desperate county?" Bo said at one point when they had stopped at a meandering creek to water their horses and relieve themselves.

"Takes a good memory," Cole replied.

"Got to ask you something."

Cole stood studying the land ahead of him, the reddish cuts and twisted guts of a land that looked as though it had been madly stirred by the hand of God himself and left to bake into odd shapes, box cañons, hidden arroyos, and everywhere confusing.

"Got to ask you if you don't aim to lead me off into this madness and shoot me in the back of the head and take my father's money, telling him I was killed by this bastard, Lucky Jack, and his boys. There'd be nothing to stop you from assassinating me and calling it an accident."

Cole looked over at him with narrowed eyes.

"You think I'd've waited this long to kill you?"

Bo shrugged. "How the hell should I know?"

"You're not much of a thinker, are you?"

"Some's given brains and others guts, guess which one I got."

"You any good with that piece you carry on your hip or is it mostly for show?"

"You want to find out?"

"You asking me if I want to test you? No, not directly. But there are those who carry a piece of iron around just for the show of it, and they're the ones who usually end up dead the quickest. Men with a gun get dumb ideas that somehow the gun makes them better than they are, going to get them what they want, going to make them boss. It doesn't. A gun's nothing more than a tool except it can get you killed quick by another fellow with a gun who knows better how to use it than you. Just wondering which one you were . . . the real thing or a false deal."

The horses raised their muzzles from the rippling brook and the water fell from them like diamonds caught in the sunlight. Bo looked about and just then a big-eared jack rabbit burst from the brush heading for its hidey hole. Bo turned and fired three fast shots, missing twice, but the third time sent the rabbit tumbling.

"That tell you what you need to know?" he said.

"Would be if the rabbit had a gun," Cole said.

"Shit," Bo said, and knocked the empty shells from his chambers and reloaded with fresh ones. "You think I never shot a man?"

"I don't even have to ask that question," Cole said, tightening the cinch on the Grulla, putting a little knee into the belly because of the way the mare would blow herself up in order to keep the cinch loose.

"I guess then you'll never know if I did or not," Bo said, following suit.

Then the two of them mounted and rode on.

After half an hour Bo asked: "How far to this Gun Town? Seems we been riding forever."

"With luck we should arrive tomorrow sometime."

As they rode along, Cole fixed a cigarette and smoked it as casually as if he'd been sitting in the shade back at his place—Woman cooking in the kitchen, the evening sky coming down, pink as watered-down blood. He wondered, too, about his boy Tom, how he was getting along being the new lawman in Red Pony. And although Cole knew the boy was tough as a tree stump, it didn't stop him from worrying. After the big fight with the Sam Starr gang, Tom had applied for the job and took it when offered. Cole hadn't objected at the time because he wanted Tom to make his own decisions, be his own man, but if he'd had his druthers, Tom would have stayed on and they would have put something together on the little ranch. If Tom had, Cole thought selfishly, Tom would be there now, looking after Woman while he was gone with the Wilsons.

"Was up to me," Bo said after a while longer, "I'd let that damn' pirate keep her?"

"Your mother?"

"My *step*mother."

"Then I reckon for her sake it's a good thing it's not up to you."

"You don't know nothing about it, mister."

"You're right, I don't, but it's a harsh way to talk about any human being."

They rode on.

After a while Bo said: "How much would it take for you to quit the game?"

"How do you mean?"

"I mean quit it. Turn your horse around and head home and forget this whole thing."

Cole drew rein. "Why would you want to buy me off?"

"I've got my reasons."

"In other words, you don't want her back. Just your daddy does."

"She's nothing to me. They've been married less than a year. Hell, she's only a couple years older'n me. Why do you suppose a young pretty woman like that would marry somebody old as my pa? You think it just might be because she wants to get her hands on his money, his holdings?"

"Cutting you out, is that it?"

Bo Wilson glared at him from under the brim of his hat, his eyes glittering like pieces of fool's gold. "I'm gonna tell you something, mister. Ain't nobody knows but me and her what she really is."

"None of my business," Cole said.

But without encouragement, Bo began to weave his tale: "She come on to me one time about four, five months after Pa showed up with her. I was out in one of the pastures, checking some fencing, and here she come riding like a man in man's britches, hardly like any lady. I knew something was up right off." He paused to see how Cole was taking all this, then continued. "She asked me to help her down off her horse . . . my pa's horse, really . . . and I did so, and when I did, she fell into my arms like it was an accident. I tried to brush her away but she clung to me, telling me what a handsome young man I was and all that. . . ."

"And naturally you couldn't resist yourself," Cole added without a hint of compassion or understanding.

"Hell, what would you have done?"

"She was another man's wife, no matter how you slice it."

"Wife! Ha. Well if she was such a good wife, what was she doing out in the pasture with me?"

Cole shrugged. He didn't care to hear the

99

tawdry tale, but the boy was full of himself now, words spilling out of his mouth like liquor from a drunkard's bottle.

"So I said to her . . . 'What the hell you doing?' . . . and she said . . . 'What's it look like I'm doing, Bo? Your father doesn't have to know about any of this.' Then she told me he couldn't do it with her any more, that there was something wrong with him inside and he couldn't get it to work. I guess now, if what that crazy doctor was saying is true, we know why it didn't work."

"I reckon," Cole said without a hint of mercy, reaching into his pocket for his makings again. He'd told himself a thousand times he was going to quit, but he just couldn't shake the urge during times of boredom or right after times of stress, and that was just about most of the time. Woman never said anything about it, but he knew she didn't care for it. He had taken to smoking outside, usually late in the evenings and early mornings with his coffee.

"Anyway," Bo continued, "she said . . . 'I love your father, Bo, honestly, I do. But a young and vital woman such as me has her needs.' Then you know what she said?"

Cole did not answer but continued to build his cigarette.

"She said . . . 'We'd be keeping it in the family, you and me. You won't be disappointed, Bo, I promise you that.' Can you believe it?"

"Boy, when you've lived as long as I have, you get so you can believe just about anything."

Cole finished rolling his shuck and searched through his pockets for a match, but was unable to dig one out. He wondered if somehow the hand of God was against him. He stuck the rolled unsmoked cigarette into his shirt pocket for later, when he might find a match.

"So I said why not and I laid her down in the grass and I gave her what she'd come for and I kept on giving it to her every chance I could and every chance she could, and I found out what sort of woman she was, and I knew she was no damn' good."

"But knowing this you kept right on. Which makes you the saint in all this?" Cole said, heeling his horse into a walk.

Bo caught up to him.

"No, I'm no damn' saint, never claimed to be, but I'm of my father's flesh and blood, and she's simply a damn' tramp trying to steal his money."

"So why not tell your father, if that's the case?"

Bo fell silent for a moment, brooding, his brow furrowed, his mouth grim. "Because I . . . didn't want to hurt him."

"Or maybe it was because you didn't want him to cast you out and cut you off for betraying him," Cole said, still wishing he had a match with which to light his smoke.

Again Bo Wilson fell into a brooding silence.

Then Cole spotted a group of Indians up on a butte, watching them. He couldn't be sure which band they were from or which reservation they'd come off of, but they sure enough were Indians of one sort or another and rarely was it good to encounter Indians in such country. The Army had licked them pretty good after the Custer debacle, had gone after them with a vengeance, and the ones they hadn't killed or captured and put on reservations had crossed over the border into Canada. But even the worst of them had eventually given up and went to the reservations. Still, little bands like those on the butte occasionally jumped the reservations now and then, taking a little revenge on the pale-faces where they could, raiding, robbing, raping, and killing more out of meanness than need. One thing about the red man, they were proud people to the bone, the younger bucks especially. They'd do a little raiding, even if it was just to steal horses or butcher a few beeves, then if they weren't caught, shot, or hanged, they'd flee back to the reservation.

Bo started to say something but Cole said: "We've got company."

"Where?"

"On that butte yonder."

"Who are they?"

"Cheyennes most likely, or Sioux, Arapahoes, Sans Arcs, or maybe even Blackfeet. Too far away to tell, but if they're a bad bunch, their arrows will sting just the same and so will their bullets, too." Cole had caught the glint of one of their brass-fitted Henrys given them as Army surplus when the new heavier Winchesters were issued to the military.

"I thought all the Indians were tamed?"

"Son, you're never going to completely tame an Indian. You might kill him or lock him up, might get him used to that government beef, but you're never going to tame him."

"So what do we do?"

"For now we just keep riding along and see if *they* do anything. But if I tell you to spur it, you spur it and run for those foothills, and hope to the Lord Jesus Christ we get there before they do."

Bo scanned the butte, counted a half dozen of them. The sat like statues for a time.

"You think they'll come after us?"

"Hard to know what's an Indian's thinking. They might, they might not. Just keep riding as if they're not there."

And that's what they did, just kept riding, and the Indians disappeared from view for a time, then came back into view, moving in step with Cole and Bo Wilson, keeping pace, nobody hurrying, just a waiting game.

The little band disappeared again, and when they reappeared, they were standing their horses directly in front of Cole's and Wilson's path, blocking further progress. Cole could see how ragged they were, half-starved-looking so that their ribs showed. They wore no war paint, nor were their horses decorated for battle.

"Now what?" Wilson said.

"Now we parlay."

One who looked like the leader wore a faded blue officer's coat, and another wore a top hat with a turkey feather in it. The rest wore plain calico shirts and wrinkled trousers. They were barefoot and dirty. The one in the Army coat heeled his horse forward to meet them, the others followed.

"We going to fight?" Wilson said out of the side of his mouth.

"No, not unless they start something first."

"Might be a bit late then."

"If it's going to be too late, it's already too late." Cole noted the beads of sweat dotting the boy's face. "Easy, boy, don't make any sudden play."

Wilson relaxed the hand that rested near his gun butt.

"What can we do for you fellows?" Cole said to Blue Coat.

He figured they'd toss some sign language at him. He knew enough to communicate some, had picked up a few words from Woman. Blue Coat grunted, said something Cole didn't understand, but pointed with his nose at their horses.

"No," Cole said firmly, shaking his head for emphasis.

Then Blue Coat pointed back in the direction they'd just come and made a plaintive sound.

"You come," said Top Hat, who had come up alongside Blue Coat. "You doctor, you come!"

"I ain't no doctor," Cole said, "and neither is this one."

"You come," Top Hat insisted with a jerk of his head. The other four watched with baleful stares. "Make medicine."

Blue Coat grunted, brought his pony nose to nose with Cole's Grulla, spoke something sharply to him, and pointed again.

Cole nodded. "OK, we come. Lead the way," he said with a flick of his hand.

"Sure as hell we're not going to go with them," Wilson said.

"Sure as hell we are," Cole told him.

"How do we know they're not leading us into an ambush to kill us?"

"They wanted to kill us, they would have tried by now."

They rode perhaps two or three miles to a small camp of half a dozen teepees, along the bank of a twisting creek. A few small campfires gave off gray threads of smoke and there was a rope remuda with a couple of dozen grass-fed ponies guarded by a pair of raven-haired Indian boys.

Those encamped came out to stare at the

returning band and their white visitors. The women set up a trilling with voices and tongues.

"What the hell!" Bo said.

"Relax, they're just glad to see a pretty white boy like you," Cole said with a devilish grin, enjoying the tough youth's sudden trepidation.

Blue Coat stopped his pony in front of one of the teepees, its outer hide smudged with smoke stains and daubed with painted circles for good luck.

"Come," Top Hat said, sliding off his own mount. "You come."

"Stay mounted," Cole told Wilson as he dismounted, and handed Wilson his reins.

Wilson looked about him nervously as the encamped people closed in around him, staring, the women still trilling, some clucking at him with their tongues.

Cole entered the teepee behind Top Hat and Blue Coat. A young woman sat cross-legged on a buffalo hide, an infant suckling at her brown breast. Cole did not stare. Blue Coat grunted something and pointed at an old woman lying on her back against the far wall, a hag of a woman with witch-like white hair and blind white eyes. She was moaning.

"You medicine man?" Top Hat said. "Treat."

"I'm not a medicine man," Cole said, remembering the medico in the wedding dress and wig and thought: *Hell, maybe I'm not, but I damned*

106

sure best make an effort here to see what ails her. He went and kneeled by the woman. Her jaw was swollen. Cole reached into the fire ring in the center of the tent and took a stick and caught flame to it and brought it close to the old woman's face.

"Easy, mother, I'm just going to have a look in your mouth."

She moaned deeply when he lifted her head. Top Hat and Blue Coat stood over him, watching intently.

Cole eased her mouth open and held the flame close to see in. He smelled the problem almost before he saw it—a rotted tooth. It obviously hurt.

"Damn," he muttered, easing the woman's head back down. He made sign language as best he could to indicate the problem with her.

"You fix," Top Hat said.

"I'm no doctor, much less a dentist," Cole said, shaking his head and shrugging his shoulders.

Blue Coat looked at Top Hat and said something, and Top Hat said: "You fix!"

Cole was momentarily at a loss, then remembered the whiskey for medicinal purposes as well as recreational purposes he always carried now tucked down in his saddlebags, or at least he hoped it still was there and that Woman hadn't found it and hidden it on him. The first time she had found it and hidden it on him, he had patiently explained: "Damn it, Woman, you never know when you might get snake bit, or something." After that she left him to his devices, or were they simply vices?

He stood and went out of the teepee, walked to his saddlebags, and dug around until he found the bottle.

"What's going on?" Wilson asked.

"Hold your water."

He went back inside and kneeled by the crone again, pulled the cork, and tipped the bottle to her mouth.

"Easy, old girl," he said, feeding her a little at a time.

"Firewater," Top Hat said, then explained it to Blue Coat. Blue Coat must have said that he wanted some, too, because Top Hat shook his head and said something harshly.

Soon as she had some of the whiskey down, Cole fed her more. It continued like that until her moaning stopped. Then he fed her still more until the whole pint was just about gone, and with it so was she, at least from the conscious world. Once passed out, Cole opened her mouth again, took out his clasp knife, and opened a blade.

Blue Coat grunted something like a warning.

Cole said: "Me fix. Yes?"

Top Hat nodded.

"You fix."

Cole pointed and said: "Fire, bring close."

Top Hat knew enough to bring a stick of flame near to the old woman's open fetid mouth to where Cole could see in clearly. Luckily the rotted tooth was near the front. Cole wiggled it with his fingers. It wobbled easily enough. He tried pulling it with just his fingers, but it was rooted on one side. He used the blade of his knife to pry it out. It came out easier than he could have hoped, and he handed the bloody thing to Top Hat. Then he spilled some of the last whiskey in her mouth to wash and sterilize the wound before putting the tip of his knife into the fire till the blade turned red hot. He touched the hot blade to the hollow just briefly, enough to cauterize the wound. The old woman jerked when he touched her with that hot blade, and he said: "Easy, mother." And quickly enough she was snoring again.

Cole stood up and held out the last few drops in the bottle to Blue Coat. The Indian slugged it down and smacked his lips, no longer looking gruff and mean as a bear.

"I fix," Cole said to Top Hat.

Top Hat looked pleased, then spoke to the woman nursing the baby who got up quickly and went out, followed by Top Hat, Cole, and Blue Coat. Top Hat signaled for Wilson to get down. Wilson looked toward Cole.

"Get down," Cole said.

"I don't much like this," Wilson said.

"Well, we're into it now, no matter what it is."

Wilson dismounted. A young boy came and took their horses after Top Hat said something.

"Hey!" Wilson said.

"Come," Top Hat said. "Eat." He made a gesture with his fingers, lifting them to his mouth.

"Guess we're staying for supper," Cole said.

"Long as we *ain't* supper," Wilson said.

Cole nearly laughed at the absurdity.

By the time the meal was in preparation, Cole had smoked three or four cigarettes and Wilson simply sat, looking nervous, watching the prettier of the squaws going back and forth. Several of them giggled at him and he didn't know what to make of it, whether or not they were mocking him or just being flirtatious. He had a peculiar feeling, being in such a strange and alien place among strange and alien people. He was uncomfortable and yet somehow fascinated by the sensation, the surroundings.

By the time the meal was served, the sky had turned a soft crimson with striated clouds, and the descending sun was throwing up the last of its light, turning the world above them into a painting.

They were served in wood bowls a stew of some sort with meat and wild onions and carrots and potatoes, the gravy thick and dark brown. They ate with wooden spoons and Wilson was surprised at how good the stew tasted until he asked Cole what he thought the meat was in it.

Cole said: "Most likely dog, or more accurately young dog puppies."

Wilson nearly gagged up what was in him. "Christ," he spewed. "Are you kidding me?"

"They serve young dog only to honored guests," Cole said. "You ought to feel privileged."

"Well, I hardly do, that's for damn' sure."

Cole spooned out the last of his bowl and said to Wilson: "You want more?"

Wilson turned green and wiped his fingers off on his pants legs.

"No thanks," he said.

But Top Hat nodded to the girl serving, a very pretty girl, the one who'd nursed the baby earlier, and she ladled more dog stew into Wilson's bowl against his objections.

"Careful," Cole said. "You insult them, and they're liable to lift your hair."

Wilson swallowed the lump in his throat, then slowly, grudgingly ate more, but slowly, very slowly.

That night they danced, and Cole and Wilson felt the air thrumming with drumbeats, the sound vibrating in their blood. The dancing went on until the wee hours, and then Top Hat led the pair to an empty teepee and said: "Go."

They entered, and Cole: "Looks like we're staying the night."

"I wish we weren't," Wilson said. "I'll tell you the truth, I don't trust these people not to kill us in our sleep."

"What, feed you and then kill you?" Cole said, stripping out of his clothes and boots, then lying down on the pallet of buffalo robes. "We'll ride out in the morning."

Next morning, they were allowed to leave the encampment. They rode on until they were several miles from the teepees. Then Bo Wilson, riding behind Cole, slipped his pistol from its holster, aimed and quietly cocked it, and pulled the trigger. The bang was loud and lonesome, and he watched Cole's hat leap from his head. Cole spilled from the saddle and landed with a thud, and did not move.

Wilson had been thinking about doing it from the outset and now had seemed the right time. He rode up to where Cole lay face down, saw his hair glisten with bright red blood.

"They can blame this on the Indians," Wilson muttered. "Either way, nobody will learn the truth. My dear stepmother will be considered dead after I report the news that she is, and if Pa ain't dead yet, he soon will be, and then me and Jesse will come into everything. Thanks for your services, John Henry Cole, but they won't be needed any more."

He holstered the pistol and rode away.

CHAPTER NINE

Rita May drove and Kate rode on the wagon seat next to her. Painted on the sides of the enclosed wagon was the advertisement for:

PROFESSOR PICKLE'S
MIRACLE #3 CURE-ALL
EXTRACTED FROM RARE EXOTIC
AFRICAN PLANTS
1 PINT $2.50
3 FOR $5.00

"You think they'll ever catch up to us?" Kate asked.

"Mine sure won't, but yours might," Rita May said.

"I tied mine up good," Kate said, uncertainty in her voice. "Still, the man's as cleaver as a weasel. What do you mean, yours won't? How can you be so sure?"

"Slim *is* a weasel," Rita May said, ignoring Kate's question.

In spite of her marital history Kate looked wounded at Rita May's words, for they both knew the truth of the matter as regards Slim Atkins, Kate's philandering husband; how he'd come over one day when Race, Rita May's husband, was away at a cattle auction and tried his best to bed Rita May with his smooth talk and fine card-shuffling hands that he put all over her.

Rita May, of course, had rebuffed his advances. And when all Slim's slick talk hadn't done the trick, he had tried to force himself upon her, exposing himself and rubbing up against her until she pulled the little two-shot Derringer she always kept in the rear pocket of her dungarees.

"If you pull any more monkey business," Rita May warned, "I'll shoot that carrot of yours off and then let's see you explain to Kate, how you come to lose it."

In an attempt to add insult to injury Slim had squawked: "Why, I wouldn't be half surprised you're a man, the way you dress and act."

"Just say one more word and I'll clip you, and, trust me, it won't feel so great, getting shot down there."

Still, Slim wouldn't let it go with just that and had threatened Rita May, that if she dared mention the incident to Kate, he'd twist the story around and put the blame on her. "And then you won't have a friend in this old world, you mannish old thing."

Rita May had given him two seconds to clear out, but he had to get one last thing said: "If I see Race coming around looking for a little vengeance, then I'll kill him, and you'll not only be mannish but a widow, too. So either way, it's just best to keep your mouth shut, woman."

She had taken aim. He had skeedadled.

But Rita May had not kept her mouth shut and had told Kate about the assault, and Kate hadn't said anything for a long time, but then she had laughed. It had shocked Rita May to hear her best and only friend laugh at her husband's attempt at infidelity, shocked and wounded her.

But then Kate had said in a serious tone: "You know something, Rita May, we women are but cursed beasts in this world, no better than oxen or sheep, and less prized than a good horse. And I for one think it's time we took matters into our own hands."

"How do you mean?" Rita May had said, surprised at her meek friend's suggestion. Kate had always been the softer and more feminine of the two, whereas Rita May was larger and wore men's clothing and kept her hair cut short and was much more the leader between them ever since Kate and Slim Atkins had moved to Disappointment Valley. Rita May's husband, Race, was a good twenty years older and was pleased to have a wife of any size and looks, just as long as she could cook, do his laundry, and share a bed with him.

The two of them had met when Rita May was working as a camp cook for a cow and calf outfit over near the Big Sandy and Race had come there to buy a bull and spotted Rita May, having a cigarette by her lonesome between meals. At first he had thought maybe she was a new hand at the place, till he had looked closer and seen she was a woman, could tell by the soft if somewhat flattened mounds of her chest beneath her wool shirt. He had walked up and introduced himself and asked did she like working the place. She had offered him a level gaze and said: "About as much as I'd like being kicked in the head by a horse."

Race had squared his shoulders and said: "I could use me a housekeeper, and it would just be me and not a bunkhouse full of waddies, and you'd have a good place to live, and I'd pay you twice what you're making here."

She hadn't had to think more than the time it took to pack a valise with her things and ride off with him into the coming winter, and by the spring he'd asked her to marry him, and she had accepted, knowing he'd probably die before she would and the house and everything else would be hers. It sure wasn't love or anything like it. Not for Rita May it wasn't.

So when Kate had spoken up after Slim had tried to assault her, Rita May was most interested in what her only friend had to say.

"I mean, Slim and Race are cut from the same wool as every other man," Kate had said, then added a confession: "Why, Race has been coming around my place every chance he gets, trying to talk me out of my bloomers. I know he's your husband, Rita May, but he's as old as dirt, and even if he wasn't I wouldn't take a married man to my bed. Fact is he was here that day Slim paid you that visit. The sons-of-bitches."

That had torn it, in Rita May's mind. Even though she wanted to hang on and collect Race's meager holdings when he passed on, she could hardly stand the thought of another round of his pawing her in the dark, his rank breath and dung-smelling skin, and how he grunted like a hog at slops every time. She was all ears, listening to Kate's complaint.

"You're right, Kate, it's time we did something about it. And you want to know something else, long as we're confessing things? I never did much care for men nohow, ever since I was a girl child. They're nothing but a bunch of dirty dull-brained creatures, descendants from apes like that fellow over in Europe claims, that Darwin fellow."

It was a rather shocking revelation for Kate who had gone to her wedding bed a virgin and with little grasp of sexuality of any sort, but to yield to her husband's demands and be the good wife to him and perform her wifely duties. Kate was a woman with very limited sexual experience.

"How do you mean you never did care for men?" Kate had said innocently.

"I was always more attracted to my own kind, even when I was little," Rita May had said. "Understand what I'm telling you, Kate?"

"I . . . I guess so."

So Rita May had done her best to explain, and as she had explained it, she had seen the color rise in Kate's cheeks.

"You mean . . . . ?"

"Yes, exactly so."

"Have you ever . . . with another woman, I mean?"

"A time or two. Before I married Race."

Now Kate's crimson coloration had turned a darker scarlet. "Oh, my!" she had exclaimed in a burst of breath.

"Look at it this way, Kate. What do women need men for out here on this frontier but to protect them and provide for them, and it seems to me that the price we have to pay for such is too high. They obviously don't love us or they wouldn't be spending every spare minute drinking, gambling, and trying to get in every gal's bloomers. So what are we truly getting out of all this except a roof over our heads and a plate of food that we ourselves have to cook, to say nothing of all the washing and cleaning and playing the rôle of whore those nights they're even home."

Kate had mused at Rita May's logic, seemed to succumb to it.

"I say we make plans to strike out on our own," Rita May had said.

Of this Kate was not quite as certain as Rita May seemed to be.

"I've been thinking about it for a long time, and now that you know the full truth about your man and me about mine, I don't see any more reason for sticking around. Hell, even if we were to stay, there's nothing to say that either one of those heathen husbands of ours might not take up with a new gal and kick us out into the streets, now, is there?"

Kate had shaken her head.

"So I say let's beat 'em to the punch."

As soon as she had seen Kate's resolve weaken, Rita May had suggested a plan of action. "At least think about it," Rita May had said, "but don't take overly long, because I've already made up my mind what I'm going to do."

Over the ensuing days they had discussed Rita May's plan, and more and more Kate was seeing the wisdom of it, feeling the sense of adventure anew, for the rosy bloom of new love had long ago worn off between her and Slim, and even though they'd only been married two years, it had begun to feel like twenty. And she could not forgive him for his attempted betrayal with her best and only friend. Anyone else, maybe, but not with Rita May.

And yet, Kate had still been uncertain until

119

one day in Kate's kitchen Rita May suddenly kissed her on the mouth. As shocking as it was, Kate knew she'd never been kissed so softly or sweetly or desirously by anyone, including Slim on his best day, and, without willing it, her body had responded in kind. And for a long full few moments neither woman had said a thing and all that could be heard throughout the house was the old Regulator clock in the parlor tick-tocking like a strong heartbeat that would never die.

"Well?" Rita May had said at last as she had waited for an answer of one sort or another from Kate.

"That's the most confusing thing that's ever happened to me," Kate had said.

"But you liked it, didn't you?"

Slowly Kate had nodded.

"I believe I did, yes."

"Do you want to try it again?"

"I can't rightly say. I feel so confused."

"Well, if you can't say, who can?"

Kate had blushed like a schoolgirl.

"That's OK," Rita May had said. "But don't let this keep you from going with me when I leave."

"When are you leaving?"

"Tomorrow night."

"That soon?"

"It's been five long years for me, Kate. I'd say I've been pretty patient. And as far as what we just did, it don't make nothing wrong with you,"

Rita May had assured. "Just makes you human and in want of tenderness and to be desired by someone who sees all the good in you."

As luck would have it the very night that Rita May had said she was to be leaving and that if Kate wanted to go with her to meet at the old churchyard in Dillon at midnight, Slim had come home drunk and started pawing at her, but before he could accomplish much of what was on his mind, he had fallen across the bed, out as cold as if pole-axed with a sledge.

Kate had tied him up good with a long length of rope she had found in the tool shed, using complex nautical knots her sea-faring father had taught her for the amusement of it when she was still a girl. She had stood for a time afterward, admiring her work, and had said to the comatose and trussed body of her husband: "I bet you're going to have a time getting loose from those."

Then, cleaning out what was left in his pockets and the saved cash from the tin box hidden behind a brick in the fireplace, she had packed a few clothes and necessaries and waited in the old churchyard for Rita May to show at the appointed hour.

The rain had been cold and wet and seemed to her an ominous beginning to their new adventure. But in the back of her mind, she was not at all sure that she was as much like Rita May in her attraction to the same sex. But still, anything had to beat living with a no-account husband.

As she had promised, Rita May had come, driving up in the patent medicine wagon pulled by a rain-slicked mule.

"Where in the world did you get this wagon?" Kate had asked as she tied on Slim's prize racer to the tailgate.

"I'll explain it later," Rita May had said. "Let's get shed of his place."

They had camped that first night ten miles out of the settlements, in among a thick grove of cottonwoods. The wagon was constructed of wood sides and a tin roof and had a door that could be locked from inside or out, depending. Inside the wagon there were stacked up several cases of the professor's miracle cure-all, a pallet of cotton ticking with two feather pillows, and some blankets in between.

"Let's shuck out of these wet clothes," Rita May had said when they had climbed in back.

They could hear the rhythmic rain pattering against the tin roof and it had sounded like someone shelling peas into a pan. Rita May had found a lantern and lit it, and their shadows had been tossed up against the walls and wavered overhead. Kate had been reluctant to undress and be fully naked in front of her friend, but finally she had relented because her clothes were so cold and wet and heavy. Together they had climbed in under the covers, shivering, and Rita May had snatched a bottle of cure-all from one of the cases, and turned down the wick of the lantern until the light winked out. They had lain there in the darkness, listening to the rain, Kate again having second thoughts about what they'd done, what they were about to do as Rita May had drunk a swig of the cure-all.

"Hmm," Rita May had murmured. "This is mighty tasty. Have you a drink. It'll take off the chill and set a fire in your blood." She had nudged Kate with the bottle.

Kate had reluctantly taken the bottle, swallowed some, and gasped: *"Ewww!* It's the worst-tasting stuff I ever drank."

Rita May had laughed softly and reached for her in the dark, and Kate had flinched. "What'd you do with Slim?" Rita May had asked.

"Tied him up in sailor's knots."

Rita May had laughed long and loud. "Sailor's knots!"

"What'd you do with Race?"

"I shot him," Rita May had said.

"What!"

"Oh, I didn't kill him, but he won't be chasing women for a good long while. Let's just say I wounded his pride."

Kate had lain, thinking, wondering. Rita May had reached out for her again.

"Rita May . . ."

"Hmm . . ."

"I . . ."

"All we have is each other now, Kate. Nobody knows but us."

"Still . . ."

"You liked it, though, when I kissed you. . . ."

"Well . . ."

"Shhh . . . drink you a bit more of this pop-goes-the-weasel, it will help relax you some, make all your troubles seem like nothing at all."

Kate had done as told, then had passed the bottle back to Rita May, and between the two of them they had eventually emptied it while listening to the rain fall and each other's breathing. After a time the rain striking down over their heads had sounded like tiny tribal drums striking something tribal in their souls. In her head, Kate had seemed to evaporate. It's all she could remember of the evening.

They had been heading west and north for ten days in a direction that the women thought they'd be least likely to be found by their abandoned husbands, or a sheriff.

Now on the eleventh day Kate said: "Look. What is that?"

Rita May pulled back on the reins, and the mule stopped.

"Where?"

"Over there."

Rita May followed the line of Kate's pointing finger.

"Looks like an animal that's been shot," Rita May said.

"I never seen no animal wearing pants and boots," Kate said. The animal's head lay under a bush, but a gray, curl-brimmed Stetson lay not far away. No horse.

"Kate, you got to stop with having men on your brain all the time."

Without waiting, Kate hopped down and cautiously approached the figure and saw that she was right.

"Is he dead?" Rita May called.

Kate found a stick and poked the man. He did not move.

"Looks like maybe he is!" she shouted.

"Then come on and let's go!"

"Well, we can't just leave him."

"What do you suggest we do, cart around a corpse?"

"We should bury him."

"Kate," Rita May said plaintively, "we got no time to be burying folks."

Kate turned and started back to the wagon, but a groan stopped her in her tracks. She turned quickly around and saw John Henry Cole trying to roll over. In the pain-filled fog of his world he'd heard voices and fought to get to them, unsure of where or who they were.

"Oh, honey," Kate said. "He's alive!"

"Just my damned luck that he is," Rita May grumbled, climbing down from the wagon. "Here we are trying to run away from men only to find a half dead one trying to entrap us."

She walked up and gazed down at Cole. "Well, he is a good-looking son-of-a-buck even for someone at death's door."

"I'll run and get some water," Kate said.

"You plan on drowning him?"

"Drink, wash his wounds."

"I suggest, instead of water, you grab a bottle of the professor's cure-all." Then, as Kate went to the wagon: "Mister, with any luck, you'll have passed over before that dear child returns and save us all the trouble of fooling with you."

Rita May saw the man's pistol dangling in his shoulder holster, his coat flapped back to expose it, and she yanked it free and hid it in her skirt folds. She sure enough didn't need an armed man around, alive or dead.

Cole opened his eyes briefly and looked up into the face of a yellow-haired woman with not a shred of pity in her plain face. Why, he wasn't even sure she was a woman. *Angel,* he thought. Who would have guessed he, of all people, would have ever stared into the face of an angel.

CHAPTER TEN

Lucky Jack grumbled and paced and mumbled in the apartment above Karl's Liberty Palace Saloon. The rain outside had chased him in off his perch and he needed a whiskey and to do something with himself. The more he paced, the edgier he became and the angrier.

"When's that dumb love-struck husband of yours coming with the money?" he said more to the fetid air in the room than to Lenora as she sat at a double-mirrored dressing table, brushing her hair one hundred strokes, though she'd actually lost track of the current number.

She watched him by way of the mirror and wondered why all the handsomest of men were the most notoriously bad to their women. But more so, why was she drawn to men like Lucky Jack, and, before him, others just as bad? Why couldn't she have been content with a man like Wilson? Even though he was nearly her father's age, Wilson had been the kindest and most caring man, and very, very generous to her. And while it was true that there was one thing he could not give her, she could always make do in other ways as many women had and would. Now take that elder boy of his, Bo, the one she'd let seduce her, or was it the other way around? No matter. It happened and she liked it, but what sort of man would cuckold his own father— nothing but a mean son-of-a-gun as handsome as a $500 racehorse. Surly and full of himself and rich, or would be once his father passed on. Why couldn't she have just worked something out with the son? Except that the son seemed to hold her in low esteem once she gave herself to him. Nothing quite ever worked out the way she'd hoped it would.

She'd always know that the chance to go on the straight and narrow, to become an honest woman wasn't in the cards for her. And now she was forever ruined by her addiction to Lucky Jack who was the worst of the bunch, and her addiction for the man was worse than opium and cocaine pills. She knew that in his mind she was little more than his personal harlot until he grew tired of her and tossed her out on the streets again, unless, of course, she could prove valuable to him in helping to gain Wilson's money and holdings.

"Well?" he demanded.

"Well what?" she said, knowing perfectly well what he was asking, knowing perfectly well, like so many times when he got like this, she had no satisfactory answers for him, because there weren't any. "Don't you already have enough money and holdings?" she said. "Do you need another five thousand out of that poor old man?"

"You can never have enough money," he said. "And besides, I've been thinking of a new plan, a better one, worth a lot more than five thousand dollars."

He paced about as was his habit when excited over something.

"I aim to kill those two idiot sons of his so you can inherit the whole kit and caboodle. I've been thinking too small here lately. Time to think big, and you're going to be right there with me. We can leave this dung heap and live like civilized folks and, as far as anyone is concerned, do it all legal. You the grieving widow and me the fellow what comes along and marries you. Hell, things go right, I might even run for Congress someday."

He seemed serious. "Well, you certainly have the soul of a politician."

He laughed. "Don't I, though?"

"Somehow I can't really see you as settled down, Lucky."

He paused and looked at her before going to the window and looking out at the needles of rain. "Maybe there's a lot about me you don't know."

She continued to brush her long hair with the ivory-handled brush. "How'd you ever get to be the way you are, Lucky?"

He turned and looked at her reflection in the mirror. "You start out as one thing, and then you become another," he said, pausing to pull a cheroot from his pocket, and then he picked a Hotchkiss match from a box on a nightstand, and struck it. "I started out honest, did all I could to do the right thing, and you know what it got me, Miss High and Mighty? It got me a dead wife and not a spare nickel in my pocket and debt up to my neck. I had to borrow the money to bury my wife. That's what being honest got me."

She watched his face growing cloudy with remembrance of the hard times.

"I was arresting and killing men who made more in one bank or train heist than I could make in a year as a lawman. So I said to myself one day . . . 'Shit, why am I wasting my time wearing this star, and for what? It's just a damn' target to show where my heart is. 'Sides, there will always be killers and thieves, rapists and throat-cutters no matter what I do.'" He blew a stream of cigar smoke into the air, watched it rise and curl against the plastered ceiling and curl back down again, a trapped cloud of pent-up frustration. "And I ain't the only one who switched sides, either. There's been plenty of others done it before and since me."

She watched his face become even more animated.

"And now you know the ballad of Lucky Jack Dancer," he said sourly.

"Yes, now I know."

"What about you? When'd you decide to take up whoring?"

"Like you said, you start out as one thing and end up another. I was a preacher's kid and later a preacher's wife, and it was all so dull and boring I just about went crazy. Then one day into our little community came a gambling man in a fine frock suit and a gold-handled cane and a smile that would stop bullets. The next thing I knew I was giving it to him like water to a thirsty man, and a week later I left town with him." A look of sadness came over her lovely features. Lucky almost felt sorry for her, except everyone had a sad story to tell as he'd learned in his days as a lawman. "Next thing I knew he'd pimped me out to men he lost card games to in order to pay off his debts. I would have done anything for Andy, and did. But as soon as I'd cleared his debts, he saw the potential in making money off me because he could charge more for me than the local cats who were mostly fat, ugly, and doped-out. But once he got a stake together, he left out the back door late one night and took every last cent we had with him." She blinked back tears. "And now you know the ballad of Lenora Adams Wilson."

"Well that's a sad tale, indeed," he said with a churlish smile. "And here all the time I thought you were a virgin and pure as the driven snow."

"You have such a way of making me feel good

about myself, Lucky," she said acerbically. "I just wonder if you'll ever stick around long enough to appreciate me before you sell me back into whoredom."

He gave a false little chuckle. "You know, I was only joking about that, just trying to get your husband to come up with some more money. I love you like horses love hay."

"What I know about men is this . . . the best-looking ones are always the worst, and there ain't a man living who won't break a woman's heart once he knows he can."

They could hear the off-footed gait of Gypsy Flynn coming down the hall, followed by a rapping at the door.

"Come in!" Lucky said loud enough to be heard.

The gimpy killer entered, his creased and crusty Stetson pulled down to the top of his ears, causing him to look like a mean streak of something.

What an ugly little man, Lenora thought.

"What is it?" Lucky asked.

"I ain't seen hide nor hair of anyone what's supposed to be bringing the money," he said. "I'm hot and thirsty, waiting down by the train station for some stranger in a suit to get off."

"You check in with Bill Hammer?"

"Did. He's in his office, shuffling through papers, as usual. Said he'd keep on."

"You get back over there and tell him to get his ass down to the train station and stand watch till you get back there. Where's Bird Brain?"

"Probably drunk."

"Go sober him up."

Lenora noticed Gypsy's viperous eyes stealing glances at her. She wore a simple wrapper and was naked underneath. She had no doubt his evil gaze could see right through her gown.

"How long we supposed to wait?" Gypsy said.

"Till I say you don't have to any more," Lucky Jack said with growing irritation.

"All right, then."

"Hit it."

The two men stared at each other for a long moment, then Gypsy said: "OK, I'm gone." He limped back out again.

Lenora involuntarily shivered. It was as though Gypsy had brought a mass of cold air into the room with him and left it there. "I truly do despise that evil man," she said.

Lucky Jack cut his gaze to her. "Saintly men do not make good killers. And here I thought you had a yen for him all this time." He flashed his wicked grin.

She turned then, away from the mirrors and glared at him. "I'd cut my own throat before I'd let him touch me."

He laughed. "I'm going down for a drink or three."

"What about me?"

"Maybe later," he said. "A man's got to have some man time."

"You mean a man needs time to whore."

He merely looked at her with cold gray eyes. "Be a good girl and stay here. You need your beauty rest."

She threw the hairbrush at him, and it crashed into the door just as he stepped out.

"Bastard!"

Such times as these left her feeling not only alone but lonely and lost, as if she'd gotten on a train with no destination and could never get off. She thought briefly about running away, but where would she go, and how could she stand life without Lucky Jack, in spite of his neglect and bad treatment of her when he was in a foul mood?

She took the small bottle with the eye dropper and squeezed several drops of laudanum onto her tongue, then got up and went over to a side table where bottles of liquor stood, poured herself a tumbler of whiskey, and drank it down. The whiskey burned her throat and like a warm snake slid down into her chest. Then she flopped down on the bed to await the sweet sensation she knew would come over her.

All is lost, she thought. She'd heard that line in a stage play once and had considered briefly about becoming an actress. At times like these she thought as an actress: *All about me is lost and I sha'n't ever be what I once hoped I'd become. I was a young and innocent girl once, oh, ever so long ago, and now I am near middle age and I can see already that my beauty is fading. Where will I be in five or ten years from now but some slattern working out of a crib?*

The thought depressed her as she waited for the drug and liquor to take effect. It would begin in her limbs, making them leaden, and then creep into her brain like fog coming in at evening across a meadow, but nothing quite so lovely as fog. She forced herself to gaze at a porcelain bird upon a shelf that Lucky had once given her—such a pretty little bluebird with its yellow beak and happy black eyes—and stopped thinking of any future. There was just the now. Just the now.

She closed her eyes and barely heard a stirring in the room, the door opening and closing, the gimpy footfall upon the carpet that slowly approached the bed.

Her eyes were still closed when she felt a hand touch her, a not so gentle touch. She whispered in her dream-like state: "Lucky . . . you've come . . . back to me."

Then the hand became rougher and there was a rank odor of sweat and horse and sweetened liquor breath and she struggled to climb out of the drowsy fog she'd fallen into, blind with panic. "What . . . ?"

Suddenly a bruising mouth smashed down upon hers, scratching her with whiskers, as his hands pulled open the wrapper she wore, like the hands of a child eager to get at candy. She did her best to ward off the attack, finally was able to open her eyes and stare into eyes that were fissured with glints of gold, not Lucky Jack's slate-gray ones.

She gasped, pushing away the mouth from hers, but now he had his hands in the places they shouldn't have been and just as suddenly she was free from the effects of the drug and the drink, but weakened by both as Gypsy Flynn forced himself on her.

He was surprisingly strong for a man his size, his wiriness aided by his lust. "You damn' tart, you've been wanting this all along, ain't you?" he growled through a set of blunt brown teeth. "Well, now you're gonna get it."

"No!" she cried, but he quickly clamped one hand over her mouth and the other around her throat.

"You struggle with me and I'll kill you!"

The filthy fingers tightened, cutting off her air. He pressed harder.

"I like 'em when they fight," he said. "Go on. Hell, I'll take you after I kill you if that's what you want. I don't mind. I done it before. Lots of times."

His voice had the cold sharp edge of truth to

it; she'd no doubt that he wasn't lying and would have his way with her dead or alive; the thought sickened her. Her air nearly gone, she stopped struggling.

"Ah, you give up too easy," he said, loosing his grip on her throat.

She lay without speaking once he took his hand from her mouth. She watched him unbutton and climb on top of her.

"What? You think you'll tell Lucky after I'm done with you and he'll come looking to kill me? You're as stupid as you are pretty, you think that."

She simply stared into his vicious eyes and only wished she had a hidden gun or knife to kill him with.

He laughed as he pushed into her, causing her to catch her breath and stifle a scream.

"Hell, Lucky don't care. Fact is he's the one told me to come on up and enjoy myself."

Her mind screamed: *No!*

He rutted into her over and over, his unwashed body rank as any man she'd ever been in contact with. He kissed her brutally the whole while, as if they were lovers. She thought about biting his face, ripping it apart until she tasted his blood, but fear paralyzed her and all she could do was lie there, still and fearful. And even though it seemed like an eternity, gratefully it was over quickly, and she thought bitterly to herself that men who did not honor women were all the same—brutes and callous cowards—and deserved nothing short of a hard death.

She did not look at him as he stood again by the bed, buttoning himself up.

"Besides, if you was to be such a damn' fool and tell Lucky anything about this and he *was* such a damn' fool as to get the idea to try and do something, I'll cut your throat and leave you to the dogs behind the butcher shop. They'll eat the flesh off your bones, and I'll do him the same as I did that Pinkerton."

He gave a short, hard laugh as he limped to the side table and poured himself a glass of whiskey and tossed it back.

"You know what that Pinkerton looked like when I slipped the dirk into his liver? My god, it was a sight to see. It had to hurt like a sum-a-bitch, getting it that way."

He set the glass down and tipped his hat as a gentleman might to a lady he'd pass on the street.

She heard him limping to the door again.

"You know," he said as he turned the porcelain knob, "you ain't even that damn' good."

She heard the door open and close, the tap, shuffle, tap of his gait dissipating, then choked on a sob that had been welling up inside her since he first laid hands on her. And the only thoughts that came flooding into her mind were all the worst thoughts a woman just violated could have. She rose from the bed and went and washed herself as best as she could from the basin on the bureau next to the chiffonier. The very act of what she'd just suffered made her ill, and her hands trembled so that water splashed and slopped over the basin. She cursed under her breath and wondered if it wasn't the sins she'd committed against Wilson most recently that she had now paid for with her flesh.

She refused to watch herself in the mirror, but could feel the puffiness of her face and eyes as she sobbed and wiped away the tears with the back of her wrist. When she finished washing, she sought again the solace of the contents in the eye dropper bottle, the rye whiskey, the blackness of night outside the window.

She locked the door and sat on the bed and mixed the laudanum with the whiskey and drank down one, two, three, and then four straight cocktails, rushing to get them down quickly.

She'd started to mix another when the conscious world became unknown to her and she drowned in a sea of blackness.

CHAPTER ELEVEN

I was sought by those who did not ask for me. I was found by those who did not seek me. I said . . . "Here I am, here I am."

In his wakeful moments John Henry Cole felt like a man being roasted over a fire. He saw the faces of angels only to lose them again in the black pit of unconsciousness. His head felt as if struck by lightning and throbbed with murderous regularity. At times he heard their voices. The voices seemed distant, as if standing on a hill, calling to him—"Mister. Mister."—and he thought he cried out: "Here I am, here I am." But perhaps it was some old Bible verse he'd read, stored away in the dusty lock box of memory.

He wanted to go to the voices and make out who they were, who called to him, but he felt nailed to the earth by a stake through his skull. He remembered briefly the lightning bolt of pain that flashed across his skull but nothing after that, not tumbling to the earth where he slammed face first, not the gritty taste of dirt in his mouth, not so much as a dream.

Rita May and Kate had lugged him beneath the shade of the wagon while the mule cropped grass and looked on casually. They daubed his head with a wet piece of petticoat Kate tore from one in her valise, and Rita May got out a finger of axle grease from a cask strapped to the outside of the wagon and applied it liberally to the scored path the bullet had taken just above Cole's right ear. Then they wrapped his head with yet another strip of Kate's petticoat, and sat back, waiting to see if he would live or he would die—one of them hoping one outcome and the other hoping for a different one.

Cole's eyes fluttered open and he winced at consciousness.

"I think he might live," Kate said.

Rita May had taken a bottle of the cure-all from one of the boxes in the wagon and sat nipping at it and ruefully watching the man. Even she had to admit, bandaged head and all, he was quite a handsome lout and said idly: "Well, he will sure enough make a pretty corpse if he don't make it."

"Rita May!" Kate said sharply, admonishingly.

"Well, he would."

"But he won't. We fixed his brokenness and it was the Lord's own hand that directed the bullet and kept it from going into his brain."

"That, or bad aim by whoever shot him."

"Give him some of the medicine," Kate said.

Rita May held the bottle up and said: "If that's true medicine, then I'm Queen Victoria." She dribbled some of the mixture into Cole's mouth.

He coughed and sputtered, thinking whoever

was pouring the stuff in was trying to drown him. He looked up into a pair of sable brown eyes that held no mercy in them, a white woman with hair, pulled back, to match her eyes, a skin white as milk, her features as spare as a low-rent hotel room, but nonetheless attractive. He shifted his gaze to the other one, prettier, but in a more girlish sort of way, her face rounder, her cheeks blushed with the color of apples just ripe for the picking.

"Well now, what do we do with him," Rita May said, "now that he's only half dead?"

"We'll keep him," Kate said.

"He ain't no darned stray dog you can just keep."

"Well, we can't just leave him out here to perish."

"He's near perished as it is. I say let Nature have it's way with him just as it has its way with all of us."

"Nature?" Kate said, finding the irony of Rita May talking about Nature when what Rita May seemed to be was something slightly against Nature, a woman's nature anyway. As for herself, she could not say, stuck as she was between the twixt and the between.

"No, we'll keep vigil over him until he either is back to health or . . ."

"Yeah, or . . . ," Rita May said, tippling from the bottle of Professor Pickle's elixir.

They fixed a meager meal and cooked it over a fire of cow pies they'd gathered after noticing a worn path of cloven hoofs that had beat the ground into dust but then wandered off into some canebrakes that certainly must have led down to water.

Cole fell in and out of consciousness, and each time he awoke, it was like somebody was using his head for an anvil to straighten horseshoes. He'd been shot a time or two before but nothing nearly as painful. He half wondered if his brain was going to leak out, and he cursed the man who shot him a thousand times over, mostly for being a poor marksman. Death would have been preferable to the pain he was suffering.

When he finally came around fully, he asked to be propped up against one of the wagon's wheels. He said to Rita May: "Sister, if you'll give me some more of that tanglefoot, I'd appreciate it."

Kate had wandered off to relieve herself in some brush near the canebrakes, leaving just Cole and Rita May to contemplate life now that they had encountered each other and neither one was overjoyed at the fact. Rita May retrieved a bottle of the cure-all and handed it to Cole who lifted it to his mouth and drained half of it straight down. Rita May had been nipping away at a bottle on her own and was feeling a nice glow that uplifted her mood somewhat. She grew loquacious now, loquacious and curious as to how it had come to be—Cole's location, face down upon the earth in the middle of nowhere.

"Sister," he said, "I was headed to Gun Town with a man I should not have trusted. . . ."

"Which would be just about every man who lives and breathes," Rita May opined.

"Maybe it would," Cole replied. "I guess he used me for target practice. It's a long story I won't bother to bore you with since you already seem a bit offish anyway."

A moment of silence and then: "Tell me about this Gun Town," Rita May said.

Cole took another pull, then propped the bottle between his knees and searched his pocket for his makings without even consciously thinking about it, pulled out his sack of Bull Durham and papers, and set to building himself a shuck.

Rita May watched him for a moment and then reached for his shaking hands and said: "Here, let me. You're about to spill all that good tobacco and what a shame since I haven't had a smoke in ages."

He watched her build two cigarettes and said: "Do you have a match or something?" He was futilely patting his pockets.

She lit them from the dying fire and handed him his. They sat smoking as a soft night wind came out beyond the canebrakes where an unseen river flowed.

"Well, it's no place a decent human being ought

to be," Cole finally said in answer to Rita May's question about Gun Town.

"Then the purpose of your going there?"

"To find a woman."

Rita May's laughter was short and sharp like the sudden shattering of glass. "What, you couldn't find a woman elsewhere?"

"Could, but not this particular one."

"Oh, a *particular* one, well ain't you the romantic."

Cole took another hit of the bottle, drew in a lungful of smoke, let it out, and watched the smoke waft away.

"I was paid to find this woman," he explained. "She's the wife of a man what got herself stolen."

Rita May nodded. "What an honorable endeavor."

"Nothing honorable about it," he said. "Just a job."

Kate returned, shifting her skirts, and joined them, sitting on the ground.

"What a lovely evening it looks like we're going to have," she said.

Kate seemed enamored of the stranger, and it rankled Rita May to think that she was.

"By the way, I'm Kate, and this is Rita May," she said.

"Name's John Henry Cole," he said.

"How is your head?"

"You mean other than the blinding pain?"

Kate smiled. Rita May did not. She wanted to find nothing charming about this man. She wanted to move on as quickly as possible and be shed of this new burden.

"Mister Cole says there is a town not far from here," Rita May said. "We will be able to deliver him to proper medical care, and then be on our way."

Kate pouted.

Cole had closed his eyes, the cure-all having taken effect.

"He's asleep," said Kate.

"Listen, we can't be dallying with this man. He says he's looking for a woman, the wife of a man. She was stolen. That means he is probably a detective, a Pinkerton maybe. We can't afford no trouble with the law."

"We haven't broken any law, have we, Rita May?"

"I reckon no judge is going to side with us for abandoning our husbands, especially since I pretty much wrecked mine's manhood. People have been thrown in jail for less."

Kate shrugged.

"We can't afford no more man trouble," Rita May said.

"I suppose you're right."

"Good. It's getting late. Let's go to bed."

"What about him? We can't just leave him out here."

"Why not? He was laying out here when we found him."

"Oh, Rita May!"

"OK. We'll put him inside."

Kate smiled. Rita May did not.

CHAPTER TWELVE

Bo Wilson concocted a fine story to tell for when he arrived back in Forty Rod, hoping upon hope that the old man had passed on and that it would be just him and Jesse to share the inheritance and whatever story he had to tell would not matter, or even be necessary, because if his father *was* dead, then the fate of Lenora would not matter and that would be the end of that and no more money would be wasted in trying to get her back.

He reined in at the Blight House and dismounted, entered, stopped at the desk in the shabby lobby, and asked: "Has my father passed away?"

The clerk looked at him with his lower jaw unhinged. He'd become worried about his chances of entering college if he could not even understand the writings of one man. The book, *Don Quixote*, he now used as a paperweight and his attention had returned to the deck of playing cards with photographs of nude women on the backs.

"No, he ain't yet, sir."

Bo glanced at the deck of cards the clerk held in his hands just below the lip of the desk and grunted disdain, then ascended the stairs and entered his father's room without knocking. His father sat in a chair by the window, looking wan with the morning light on his features. Jesse lay sleeping across the bed. Dawn had been in progress less than an hour and the sun was not yet fully risen above the edge of the horizon.

Wilson, always a restless man, had had a dream about his young wife, that the two of them had been riding horses and that he'd fallen off. He'd called out to her to come back, but she only laughed and kept riding and he knew in the dream that he would die alone. He'd awakened and rose from the bed and went and sat by the window. He'd seen Bo come riding up alone and it troubled him greatly. *Don't tell me that Mister Cole has perished the same as the Pinkerton,* he thought wearily. *My God, am I snake bit when it comes to finding my Lenora?*

"You feeling better?" Bo said. His wish for learning his father had become a corpse had not borne fruit. "It looks as if you are."

"I am, somewhat, yes."

The elder Wilson looked toward the door expectantly. "Where's Mister Cole? I saw you ride in alone."

Bo shook his head, taking off his hat and running a forefinger around the inner hatband to wipe dry the sweat. "Tell the truth, Pa, he's no longer among the living, Mister John Henry Cole ain't."

Wilson turned his head to look at his older boy, his eyes stricken with concern.

"What happened to him?"

"Lucky Jack killed him."

Wilson lowered his gaze, his head dipped down.

"No," he said. "I can't believe it. How?"

"We caught up to that killer and his bunch but they had us outgunned. I can tell you this if it makes you feel any better. Cole went down brave, fighting to the last . . . bravest man I ever saw. I barely escaped with my life."

The father wondered at the veracity of the tale but he had no sound argument against it.

"And there's more bad news I've come to deliver, Pa."

Wilson raised his head again, his eyes boring into those of his son.

"Your dear wife has also perished. Lucky Jack killed her soon as he realized me and Cole had come to get her. Cut her throat ear to ear. I witnessed the whole thing. It's what set off the gun play. Lots of blood shed over that woman."

"Except for yours," Wilson said, his lips trembling, his voice quavering with a mixture of pain and anger.

"Look! I done my best, Pa. You can't ask more of me than that."

Jesse roused from his sleep and sat up and said: "What is it? What's happened?" He looked

150

toward his brother who now held his creased hat in his hands.

"I just told Pa that Lenora is dead," he said. "So is Cole. Lucky Jack and his boys killed them both."

"But then how was it you got away?" Jesse said in all innocence.

It jerked Wilson back from the fog of grief to present reality, that simple question, for it was a question he had hesitated to ask but had wanted more than anything to know.

"I'll tell you how," Bo said, for he had worked the story and worked it until he had sharpened it to a fine point. "After they killed Lenora, there was a shoot-out. When I saw there was no chance to do more, I ran like hell. I'm not ashamed to admit it. Bullets were whizzing past my head like a nest of angry hornets set loose. I killed a couple of them and might have wounded one or two more, but there were just too many to fight them all." Bo lent a dramatic pause to give the tale time to soak in, then continued. "Cole led us right to Lucky Jack's camp and for a time I thought we were going to be successful in getting our dear stepmother back, for those two men seemed to know and like each other well enough, and it seemed at first Cole could likely work something out. We all sat and had a few drinks and discussed it, and Cole was pretty convincing of the futility of keeping Lenora. Lucky Jack seemed to agree and called his men to bring her out. And then with a wicked grin, he swiped her throat with a straight razor, and when he did, Cole drew his piece and the firing all around commenced, for we both knew that if we didn't fight our way out, we'd be as dead as she was."

"Stop!" Wilson said. "I don't want to hear any more of this."

Bo clamped his mouth shut, glanced at Jesse who sat bug-eyed on the edge of the bed, his stocking feet dangling, a toe poking through the end where it had worn through the sock. He reminded Bo of a beguiled urchin.

"I will never get that image out of my mind," said Wilson obviously distressed.

"Sorry," Bo said, "but I thought you'd want to know how things went down. I blame myself for our failure."

His father's squinted eyes had come to rest on Bo.

"You das'n't blame yourself," he said. "You did what you could."

But Bo detected the disappointment in the old man's voice and it angered him even more.

"I'm glad at least to see that you survived your ordeal," Wilson added.

"Yes, but what did I survive it for if I could not return your treasure?"

Jesse thought that his elder brother was as usual being overly dramatic, trying to cull more favor with their father than he deserved and he felt a pang of jealousy now that Bo seemed the center of attention.

"We should head back as soon as you're up to traveling," Bo said. "I imagine our ranch operations have gone all to hell without us there to watch over things. You know how Cullen can be when he gets wound up tighter than a two dollar watch on liquor."

"Cullen is a good man," Wilson said.

"For a ramrod, maybe. But you and I both know that there ain't no man going to attend another man's business in the same way he would his own."

"You never did like him much, did you?"

"He's a mean drunk."

"Only when he's not working."

"Someday he might disappoint you the same way I have."

Wilson looked at his cantankerous but beloved son, then at his other, more quiet and genteel son who would never be able to take over the ranching operations once he'd passed because he lacked the grit to take charge and order other stronger men around. Bo had just enough meanness and lack of compassion in him to see that the work got accomplished.

"You've not disappointed me, Bo," he said wearily, rising from his chair. "You and Jess are my only flesh and blood, the only ones to

153

carry on the family name. A father can never be disappointed in his sons."

Jesse said nothing but instead reached for his boots and stuffed his feet down into them as they made preparations to leave, gathering up what few things they had in the room.

"I think we should hire a hack for me to ride in to the nearest railroad town," Wilson said.

Bo nodded in agreement and Jesse followed suit.

They were just descending the stairs when met by the odd Doc Pursewater.

"Howdy, gents," he said, now dressed in the garb of a Zouave soldier with gold-trimmed blue blouse and baggy chasseur pantaloons. "Just back from the Crimean War, and, oh, we whipped them Huns good, we did. Didn't suffer so much as a bloody scratch though all around me comrades were falling like rain. The good news was I met and had a brief affair with Florence Nightingale herself, in my tent on quiet evenings. She'd appear exhausted and I'd invite her in and we'd dine on sturgeon roe and oysters and wash it all down with the finest champagne. My, oh, my, but what a passionate woman, though my lips are forever sealed on the intimate details." He made as if to lock his lips with an invisible key. "And how is my patient today?"

"Fine," Wilson lied, noting the madness of the man, while having privately to admit that there were probably worse physicians on the frontier if not stranger ones.

"Well, then, I take it you are leaving, against my best advice for several more days of bed rest?"

"You take it correct," Bo Wilson said, brushing past the medico and down the rest of the stairs where he stopped at the desk and paid the room bill and asked the location of the nearest town that had a railway station.

"That would be Gun Town, fifty miles west of here."

"All well and good," Bo said. "But what's the next town other than that one?"

"Why you'd have to travel an extra forty miles down to Buffalo City." Looking at the elder Wilson easing down the stairway in the company of that crazy Pursewater, he added: "Your kin don't look like the extra forty miles would do him no good. Was my pap, I'd ride him on to Gun Town and catch the Union Pacific flyer."

"Well, he's not your pap," Bo said coldly, "so mind your own business."

The clerk's mouth snapped shut like a sprung mousetrap as he put the room payment into a tin box and then busied himself with the ledger book as if looking for the name of somebody important. The most important person to have ever passed through town was White Eye Anderson who'd helped bury Wild Bill Hickok and then told the story to the boys at Bulldog Ike's saloon late one evening while drinking his fill of free drinks just for the privilege of knowing the notorious gunfighter. The desk clerk had been among the audience to hear White Eye's tale. And though the clerk had seen many strangers come and go, he'd yet to understand why a fellow so ill would want to travel an extra forty miles over rough country instead of going to a nearer town. He pulled from a lint-filled pocket a plug of tobacco and sliced off a chunk with the blade of a small stag-handle clasp knife and stuck it in his cheek as he watched the trio go out the door.

Doc Pursewater stood in the center of the lobby, looking resplendent and quite incongruous in his baggy blue trousers. *Well, at least he isn't the Widow Delia today,* the clerk thought, chewing on the plug trying to soften it.

"Quite an odd group of fellows," Pursewater said with all seriousness.

"Look who's calling the kettle black, Doc?" the clerk replied.

Pursewater didn't seem to take offense at the slight. "Well," he said, "I've got to go and treat Emile Wurst's shoat pig. Emile says it's slinging snot from its nose and won't let him near it. Says it damn' near ripped off Gerta's leg when she tried to slop it. Says it might have a bad case of screwworm, about which I'd agree having heard the symptoms."

"That or demons has entered it," opined the clerk.

"Demons!" Pursewater being a man of science was not a proponent of such things as demons and talking snakes and whales that swallowed humans and spit them out again. "Demons! Now why the hell didn't I think of that?" he said. "I'll go right off, and if that's what it proves to be, I'll come get you and you can exorcise them."

"I don't reckon no matter how fat pigs get they need no exercising, Doc," the clerk said smugly.

"Not exercise, you nitwit . . . oh, hell, just forget about it."

The clerk watched the medico exit, shook his head, spit into the brass cuspidor at his feet, and said with no degree of sympathy: "Crazy son-of-a-bitch."

CHAPTER THIRTEEN

They sat with their backs against the wagon wheel while Rita May built a cigarette and smoked it and looked up at the star-salted sky.

"Do you think we've done the right thing, Rita May?" Kate asked.

"What . . . about him?" she said with a jerk of her head to the man inside.

"No, I mean about leaving our men?"

"Well, I sure as hell did, didn't you?"

Kate shrugged. "I'm sort of getting lonesome for a man, if you know what I mean."

"I thought I'd be enough for you, but I reckon not, is that it?"

"Oh, no, Rita May, I didn't mean it that way. But no matter how we want to slice it, it's not the same without a man."

"I guess if you don't mind being rooted around on like you were slops at a trough, it ain't." Rita May reached for a newly open bottle of the cure-all and tipped it to her mouth, then smacked her lips loudly and on purpose before handing it to Kate. "Time will come you'll see that a man ain't worth the trouble and that you'll like a lot more being able to take care of yourself."

"Still, what about him?"

"What in God's name do you intend on doing with him, Kate? It ain't like he's some dog we found you can just up and keep."

Kate felt somehow mournful, thinking that the man inside the wagon would soon enough depart their company.

Rita May noticing Kate's mood, made a ribald joke that caused Kate to laugh.

John Henry Cole had woken and now listened to them talking, their laughter, and was comforted by the sound of friendly voices even though his head still throbbed with vicious intensity. *An inch over,* he thought, *and I would have been dead. I wonder why I ain't?*

The two women sat until they'd emptied the contents of the bottle and Kate flung it off into the night where it hit with a hollow thud.

"Well, I'd say its time to turn in, Kate."

"What about him, we can't just leave him out here, to the wolves and such?"

Rita May glanced at Cole who lay on his side, a ratty blanket over him. "Wolves ain't going to eat him, don't be foolish."

"They might, if they get hungry enough."

"Oh, don't be a twit."

They'd heard howling off in the low hills earlier, a sound like ghosts walking around calling to one another, ghosts who were lost and looking for something, Kate had said at the time. A not unfriendly argument ensued between them about the possibility of being eaten by wolves until Rita May threw up her hands.

"OK, OK, we'll take him inside the wagon with us if it'll please you."

"It will."

Together they helped him into the wagon.

"He's as heavy as a damn' steer," Rita May complained as Cole's world gave out on him and things went dark and silent.

Once they'd wrestled him in, they stretched him out on the pallet. Kate began tugging off his boots, wrinkled her nose as she did.

"He's a bit ripe," she said.

"You just now noticing?"

"We'll need to strip him out of his duds, too, and wash them tomorrow."

"Suddenly you're Florence Nightingale," Rita May said.

"Who?"

"Never mind."

They stripped him down to his skin and both women did not hurry in covering him with a blanket but instead pretended to await the other one.

"He's beautiful." Kate sighed.

"He's got a bunch of scars," Rita May countered. "Like all he's done his whole life is fight and get shot and stabbed."

Tossing his coat, something fell out of an inner pocket and rang against the floorboards like a large coin. Rita May held the lantern close and took it up between her fingers.

"Jesus!" she said. "He's a damn' lawman."

Kate examined the badge closer. "What'll we do?"

"Git shed of him as soon as we can. But first, we need to hide that damn' pistol hanging from his holster."

In the outer dark the wolves continued to call to one another and the sound of them sent shivers through Kate once they'd accomplished their aims, Rita May hiding the Colt inside a half-filled box of cure-all.

"Nothing more to be done for tonight," Kate said, and shucked out of her clothes and climbed in next to Cole.

"What the hell you doing?" Rita May demanded.

"Getting some sleep. You coming?"

The yellow glow of the lamp cast them in shadows and light like some ancient and rare painting of urchins upon the plain, lost and weary. As it appeared to the stars and the mule cropping grass shoots, a lone wagon had come to rest in a land so far and distant from anyone or anything, it may well have been a sailing vessel, beached upon a sea of grass.

"Christ." Rita May sighed, sliding in on the other side of the naked man. "This just feels all wrong."

Kate said nothing, drowsy as an old hound in the sun, her right hand resting on Cole's chest. She felt warm and safe against the stranger in a way she would not have been able to explain. The rise and fall of Cole's chest was soothing to her.

Rita May, on the other side, was both confused and irritated at the situation. Not unlike Kate, she, too, found a certain attraction toward the man, and also like Kate could not begin to explain it. She never before had been much attracted to any man and all had proved worthy of her disdain, but somehow, strange and odd as it seemed, she felt different toward John Henry Cole.

Still, she told herself, the man had a badge on him, and as far as she was concerned he was dangerous. *Damn it to hell,* she thought. *Damn it to hell.* She felt him shudder in his sleep and instinctively reached a hand out to touch him, to calm whatever nightmare or pain he might be having. His skin was hot but not fevered, his limbs and chest muscular, hard as hickory. Without willing it, she lightly traced her fingertips over the smooth scars welted over his body.

In the darkness the three of them lay, strangers with uncertain futures, Rita May's thoughts as twisted as tree vines. She could hear Kate's purring snores, Cole's heavy breathing. She

162

closed her eyes, wishing for sleep to come, to rush time, knowing and believing as she did that the sooner they got rid of the stranger the better off everyone would be. Then, too, she thought, what if whoever had shot him was to come back and find her and Kate harboring the man?

Suddenly his hand reached out and cupped her breast, and she flinched and removed it, nearly vociferating, but then realized that he was still asleep. Moments later he whispered the word—"Woman."—then fell silent again.

The unexpected touch was what she imagined being touched by lightning would be like, and the bolt of it traveled through her blood, hot and unwanted. She lay as stiff and still as a corpse, and eventually fell into a light sleep.

During the night John Henry Cole opened his eyes and felt the presence of both women beside him. His head felt like an old bullet, rattling around in a pan. He realized, too, that he was naked, while they were clothed, and thought with a macabre sense of humor that it was just his luck to be sandwiched between two women and his head hurting so bad he could not even think of all the possibilities.

He eased himself from between them. Every movement caused his throbbing brain to remind him what a bullet creasing the skull feels like. He fumbled about in the dark until he found his shirt and trousers, and tugged on his trousers, then his shirt, and eased open the back door and climbed out.

He stood for a moment, trying to gain his balance in the black night with naught but a million stars to look down upon him. He plucked the sack of Bull Durham from his pocket and with great effort fashioned a bad cigarette, then found a single match and struck it on the iron rim of a wagon wheel, cupping the flame until the cigarette caught fire. He snapped out the match and but for the glow of the end of his cigarette and the stars above, the land was dark as the soul of a bandit.

His head felt as heavy as a river boulder but he stood and smoked and gathered his memory from when Bo Wilson had shot him, how they'd left that Indian encampment, the old woman with the bad tooth, the dog dinner. *You'd think that boy had nothing to complain about,* Cole thought. *But the son-of-a-bitch saw reason to back-shoot me.* Cole's anger grew nearly as hot as the end of his cigarette. He thought about his own boy, Tom, what all he had gone through and how he turned out good in spite of it. He wondered if Tom was all right, in his bed sleeping, possibly with a woman of his own now that he'd become his own man. *Damned fool kid,* he thought with slight amusement, *nearly gets killed in Red Pony and ends up taking the marshal's job there.* "I hope you're all right, boy."

"Who're you talking to?"

Cole turned and there stood Rita May wrapped in a blanket. She'd listened to Cole get up, listened to him dress, and ease out of the wagon. She felt compelled to talk to him alone, out of earshot of Kate.

"Oh," he said, surprised he had not heard her, wondering if getting shot in the head messed up his instincts so badly a body could sneak up on him so easily. "Didn't even realize I was talking. It was to my boy, I reckon."

"You have a son, then," she said. "Means you're married?"

"Was, a long, long time ago. But she died."

Somehow this was the answer Rita May was hoping to hear.

"Found the badge," she said. "What's a deputy marshal doing way out here?"

He drew on his smoke, exhaled. "I ain't one no more. That was a long time ago, too."

"If you're not, then why do you carry that badge?"

"Sentiment, maybe."

"That's hard to swallow."

He looked at her. "You want to smoke?"

"Sure, why not."

He handed her his makings, and watched as best as a man can watch a woman in darkness make a cigarette, then lit it off his. She exhaled a stream of smoke.

"Sometimes it comes in handy, too, the badge."

"Like if you're looking for someone and need to impersonate a lawman?"

"Yeah, like that."

"So who are you looking for?"

"Was," he said with emphasis.

"Was," she said.

"That man who hired me to get his wife back I spoke of earlier. Most likely would have, too, but then his boy shot me."

All of it sounded too familiar to Rita May, but she wanted to know more about just what sort of fellow she was dealing with. "Why'd his son shoot you?"

"Long story, but let's just say he didn't want his mother back . . . stepmother, I mean. He didn't want her to come in on the money. Money's always a good reason to get rid of somebody."

"That somebody being you?" she said as she leaned against the side of the wagon, the blanket held tightly around her.

"Me and his stepmother," Cole said. "Kill two birds with one stone. Only he didn't kill this bird, and that was his mistake."

"You aim to find him and kill him?"

"I do."

"You're a hard man."

"When I have to be, yes."

Inside the wagon Kate had awakened, discovered the two of them missing, started to rise

166

off the pallet, but then stopped when she heard them outside. As she listened to the murmuring sounds they were making, her heart sank like a cold stone tossed into a river.

Later Rita May returned alone into the wagon, being careful not to wake the already awakened Kate, and slid down beneath the quilt.

"I heard you two outside," Kate said softly.

"We'll be shed of him soon as we get to that next town," Rita May said.

"You promise?"

"Yes, I promise, now let's get some sleep."

"Will you put your arms about me?"

Rita May drew Kate close and held her, and together they fell asleep that way.

Outside, Cole sat smoking a cigarette and thinking about Woman. He finished his smoke and lay down and closed his eyes, weary as a government mule working two hundred acres of cotton land. He slept.

When he woke again, it was to the bouncing of the wagon over a rutted track, the clinking of the bottles of cure-all in their cases. How he'd ended up in the back of the wagon again was a mystery. He had no memory of it, but there he was and he reckoned the women were up front, driving. His head still hurt like hell and the rest of him didn't feel too good, either.

Later, when the wagon stopped, he climbed out and sat, cross-legged, on the ground while the women were busy fixing lunch. There was no tension among them, but each of them went about in silence, Kate baking biscuits in a Dutch oven and frying a pan of sliced bacon after Rita May gathered cow pies for fuel.

Rita May and Kate both avoided looking directly at Cole, and he felt foolish simply waiting for the women to fix the meal, so he stood up and wandered off a ways, trying to get his bearings, at least to spot a known landmark to tell him how far out from Gun Town they were. They'd not followed a road but had gone across country and it was confusing to him because every rock and arroyo looked the same as every other. He was not sure if he knew the exact direction that they should be heading, hoped it would come to him. His head hurt only slightly less than the day before.

"I think we must be lost," Rita May said when later they stopped by a creek and unharnessed the mule for a rest and water.

Cole took in the landscape and said: "No, we're not lost."

"How can you be sure?"

"You see that set of hoodoos yonder?" pointing with his chin.

"Hoodoos?"

"Those funny-shaped spires of rock."

"Yes."

"Well, that's what we used to call the Devil's Fork. Gun Town is just beyond. We'll be there come evening."

Kate remained silent, and Cole realized he would be glad when they parted company. What he didn't need, he told himself, was woman troubles when he already had a hatful of troubles as it was and they both seemed irritated by his presence.

The sun had already begun to sink and looked like a blood ball melting into the earth. The wind was a dead thing and the land was silent but for the creek water whispering over stones.

They waited around for a time, then Cole helped Rita May hitch the mule into its traces and it brayed a protest against such indignities.

"Ask you something?" Cole said as he drew the final hitch.

"What?"

"How'd you come by this rig, anyway?"

"None of your damn' business."

He watched her stalk off.

Women! he thought ruefully.

CHAPTER FOURTEEN

As they traveled toward Gun Town, a dark thought entered John Henry Cole's mind: *What if that son-of-a-bitch, Bo Wilson, decided to go back to the cabin and take the money Wilson had given in advance? But worse, what if he did something to Woman in the trying? She was capable of defending herself, more than capable, but what if . . . ?* He began to brood over these possibilities. Any man who would shoot another in the back over nothing at all was the sort of fellow who was capable of anything and the thought of Bo Wilson molesting, perhaps killing Woman ate at his guts. He wanted to hurry and get to Gun Town and send a telegram to Woman to alert her of the possibility that Bo would come for the money, and maybe for her.

It was around the hour of midnight that the trio with the medicine wagon pulled into Gun Town. There was a checkerboard of light along the main drag coming from the saloons and whorehouses—those of the honest businesses were dark.

Kate gasped and said: "Oh, my!"

Rita May saw where she was looking. Lying in one square of light as greasy as old butter lay the bodies of two men just inches apart, one face down, and the other face up. An hour before their arrival the two men had shot each other over a prostitute that neither could afford, having drunk up all their wages previously. They had been bum-rushed outside by one of the burly barkeeps and told to stay out. They had blamed each other for their impoverished state of affairs. Both were graveyard dead in less time than it took to toss back a shot of tanglefoot, and were still just as dead when the medicine wagon passed them by. Nobody had come at the sound of the gunfire because gunfire was as common an occurrence in the town as whores wearing feathered hats and keeping cats for pets.

Cole, who had driven the last few miles under a full moon, did not halt the wagon but drove it on past the corpses.

"Don't look," Rita May said to Kate. "Best to ignore the worst of what you see in this life and pretend you never saw it at all." Privately Rita May was worried that Kate might find life in yet another shot man.

"But . . ."

"Get on, mule," Cole said in agreement.

"But aren't you going to do something, Mister Cole?" Kate asked.

"Not to worry," he replied. "They won't hurt you. They're dead."

Rita May stifled a smile even though the source of her humor was macabre.

Once beyond the dead men, Cole pulled reins and called—"End of the line, ladies!"—and stepped down.

Kate nearly said what was on her mind, about not wanting Cole to leave just yet, but didn't. Rita May merely sat there, tight-lipped, the reins now threaded between her fingers. She knew that no matter what, it was best to keep on moving toward a destiny she had dreamed for herself and Kate, but worried now the dream might turn into a nightmare.

Cole said: "I want to thank you both kindly for hauling my bacon here. I might have died out there . . . not from the bullet but from being left afoot. I owe you a debt of gratitude."

"Good luck, Mister Cole," Kate said.

Rita May remained silent, staring straight ahead. She prepared to snap the reins over the mule's weary backside but was interrupted when Cole said: "There once was a good hotel here, if you-all choose to spend the night, maybe get a decent meal. It's yonder, just up the street. Was the biggest building in town and still might be. Can hardly miss it."

Rita May waited a beat, then said: "I suppose you'll be staying there yourself?"

"Probably so, for the night at least. But I aim to leave on the flyer tomorrow, whenever it comes in."

"Going home again?" Kate wondered.

"Yes."

"I suppose you have a wife?" Kate said.

"Well, I have a woman, but I'm not married to her."

Rita May snapped the reins and shouted: "Git along there, mule."

Cole stood and watched the wagon continue up the street. His needs were few and simple—a steak, perhaps a little good whiskey, and a comfortable bed, in whatever order he could find them. He entered the very saloon in front of which he had dropped off the wagon.

The interior was a noisy, cramped, and smoke-filled room of loud voices, curses, dance-hall girl laughter, and general midnight mayhem. No matter what town a man was in, certain things could be counted on—night crawlers, bruised egos, hearty lust, unquenchable thirst, the general need to commune with like-minded humans. Except for the loners. And there were always the loners who came merely to drink, to study themselves in the backbar mirrors. Some such men stood alone and apart at the end of the bar while others stood in bunches, laughing and voicing opinions about everything under the sun. Some played poker and some waited their turn with the working gals who always did a brisk business on Friday and Saturday nights. Cole wasn't sure which night this was and didn't care. He found a spot at the bar and ordered a whiskey.

When it was poured, he asked the barkeep if there was a doctor hereabouts.

"What?"

"A doctor. Is there one in town?"

The barkeep nodded his blockish head and pointed with his nose toward a corner of the room. "Got one. That's him. Your lucky day."

Cole saw an elderly man with a tart propped on one knee, a tart young enough to be the old boy's granddaughter. He worked his way over to the table through the bunched crowd of cowpunchers and other dusty types and was quickly appraised by the old boy with the tart on his knee.

"I'm told you're a doctor!" Cole shouted above the din.

The medico's creased and aged features looked like they'd been sculpted by wind and rain and bitter disappointment. The girl, while pretty at a distance, showed buckteeth when she smiled, pitted cheeks beneath face powder and rouge.

"I usually don't patch on weekends!" the old man shouted, then gave the girl's waist a squeeze.

"I can pay," Cole said.

"What'd you do to get that?" the medico asked, glancing at the bloody bandage wrapped around Cole's head.

"I didn't do anything. It was done *to* me."

"That's the way it works out half the time."

The girl smelled of perfume and sweat, her hennaed hair more bronze than red.

"I'm sort of busy right at the moment," the doctor said in a croaking voice, smiled and pinched the gal until she playfully slapped his hand away. It had begun to creep closer to her bosom.

"What about when you finish up?" Cole suggested.

"You offering to pay in cash or chickens, something like that?"

"Cash."

"Let's have a look at you."

"Here?"

"Good as any place, and I don't have to lose my turn with young Lindsey here."

Cole unwrapped the bandage and leaned his head down.

"I'll need to clean it out and sew it up."

"Suits me down to my boots. Can you do it now?"

"Another hour of waiting won't kill you, and if it does, I couldn't have done you no good anyhow."

"Some place I could buy a decent meal while I'm waiting for an opening in your dance card?" Cole said, glancing at the girl who flicked her tongue at him like a serpent on the hunt.

"Down the street. German woman stays open

all night for the drunks' business, if you don't mind bratwurst and sauerkraut."

"Beats trail grub," Cole said.

"Not so sure about that."

A man came in with a monkey on a leash that was wearing a little coat and with a fez on its grinning head, baring its teeth at everybody. It carried a tin cup while the fellow cranked the handle on a music box. The pair was a real show stopper, the monkey going about the gathered crowd, holding out the cup for coins.

"Now there's a son-of-a-gun who's figured it out," said the physician. "Don't have to do nothing but crank the handle on that music box and feed that monkey peanuts for doing all the work."

"Oh, look, ain't it cute?" the tart said.

"Which," the medico said, "the monkey or the grinder?" Then he laughed and showed large yellow teeth beneath a mustache stained the color of urine on snow.

The pair of them laughed while Cole made his exit, avoiding the grinder and the monkey altogether.

Outside, the night was in full swing, and Cole made his way back up the street to that point where the corpses still lay undisturbed. The one that had been lying face down was now lying on his back like his companion and their socked feet pointed toward the star-filled sky. Someone had stolen their boots and turned out their pockets.

Cole found the diner more by its scent of cooking sauerkraut than by any other sign, just a simple little place with a lonely couple of lit gas jets on the inside.

A large, aproned woman sat alone, smoking a cigarette over a cup of whiskey-laced coffee, the bottle propped next to the cup, twin braids the color of faded ropes snaked atop her head, her ruddy face a mask of stoicism.

A bell over the door tinkled when Cole entered, and she looked up. "*Ja*, come in."

"I thought I already was," Cole said, closing the door behind him.

She looked at him quizzically, then snorted like a blue shoat trying to muscle its way to the slop trough. "Is a joke, *ja*?"

"Yes," he said, and sat down at one of four or five empty tables. "I'd like something to eat, please."

"*Ja, ja*, vat you have, eh?"

She smelled of flour and yeast, wild onions, and sweat as she left her spot to come and stand over him. She was heavy in the prow, the top of her faded gingham dress appearing to be stuffed with small pillows.

"A steak would be good," he said. "Coffee."

"Just *der Kraut* and *der Frankfurters* is all what I got," she said.

"OK, make it that."

"Good, *ja*," she said, and waddled off toward an open kitchen.

She returned with a plate stacked high with sauerkraut and two fat sausages, then returned with a pot of coffee and a cup.

He wolfed down what was on his plate while she watched.

"How much?" he said, reaching for the pot of coffee.

"Two bits, eh? You vant more?"

"No thanks."

He eyed the smoldering cigarette she'd left in a glass ashtray.

"Don't suppose you'd sell me one of those," he said.

"*Ja*," she said, and went and built him one and came back with it and the bottle of liquor she'd been nursing, and refilled his coffee cup leaving enough room for a hit of the liquor. "Maybe we talk, you keep Gerta company, till the drunks stumble in, *ja*?"

"Sure," he said.

She lit his cigarette, and then sat across from him. They smoked and drank. He asked her about her life, how she'd come to this place, and from where. An hour passed in idle chat. The woman's liquor had rubbed off the rough edges of his pain while he listened to her slip in and out of English, telling about a farm in Ohio and a father who beat her mother and siblings so bad that one night she attacked him in his sleep with a rake. She laughed, loud and hearty, at the memory, chirping: "I got him pretty good, *der Papa*."

She spoke also of a twin sister who had been kicked in the head by a horse and never got any older than seven even though she had lived half a century by the time she'd died in her bed.

"I had *der* husband, too," she said, her ruddy cheeks as dark as beets. "*Herr* Schmidt. He vas goot to me until he got smitten with a *Liebchen* who come around selling her papa's milk. Ha! Off run Franz like a *Kind* after *der* sweet candy. Only it was no candy he vas after but the *Liebchen*'s sweet milk!" The booming sorrowful laughter filled the room again.

She poured the last of the liquor into their cups and made them each another cigarette.

"No more men fer Gerta! Men no ting but *der* trouble."

After several more minutes of just plain silence, the medico came in, his gait slightly unsteady.

"There you are," he said, and came and sat down at the table.

"Fritzy," he said to the woman, "I don't suppose you have any apple strudel left over?"

"Maybe. I go and see, *ja*."

She stood from the table like a lumbering beast and trundled off toward the kitchen.

"That woman makes the best strudel in all the

West," the medico said. "Name's Doc Pursewater, by the way."

"You look familiar," Cole said, seeing the man now in a light not clouded by cigar smoke.

"I think I'd remember you," Pursewater said. "I'm good with faces even if I'm not so much with names. I don't remember your mug."

"Funny, but you look like another sawbones I met not long back, only he was a tad nuts. Wore a wedding dress the first time I met him."

A slow wry smile formed itself under the dirty yellow mustache.

"Probably my brother Calvin," Pursewater said. "He's a brilliant medicine man, but has a few gears missing their teeth."

"A *few?*"

"Well, perhaps more than a few. My father once caught him making love to our old cow, Bess. The old man near beat him to death with his razor strap over it and sent him away to live with a couple of my crazy as hell aunties. I think that's where Cal got his leanings, if you know what I mean."

Gerta brought a bowl of steaming strudel and set it before Pursewater who attacked it with his spoon as if he had a train to catch and was already ten minutes late.

Gerta and Cole looked on.

When finished, Pursewater said: "Yum. Now let's walk over to my office and let me clean that head wound and see if you might have got an infection started in it."

The nighttime hour now seemed lonelier than ever when they stepped outside again, the air blacker, the cacophony from the watering holes more subdued as the night crawlers realized that the hour was drawing near when they'd have to crawl back to whatever place they called home. It was the hour when the last hand was played, the last pot raked in, the last shot tossed back, when cowpunchers mounted their ponies, and when a man couldn't wait to do it all over again.

It was a deep dark night awaiting the first gray of dawn that seemed forever in coming except to those who slept a dreamless sleep, those who knew they'd have to touch their feet to cold floorboards and rise and head for the outhouses, then scrape whiskers from their face, and eat a breakfast of biscuits, mush, and bitter black coffee. And in that coming dawn's hour, when everything seemed new again and full of fresh hope, was when priests prayed and birds lined telegraph wires like old men swapping tales, and the first wagon or horseback rider had not disturbed the road yet. And for a very short while the world would seem safe from violence because even the murderers had to sleep sometimes.

Cole and Pursewater went up the street and once more past the dead men.

"What about them?" Cole said.

"Can't do a thing for 'em," the medico said.

"No, I mean, how long will they just lay there before somebody does something, haul them to the undertaker or bury 'em?"

"Oh, I imagine Marshal Hammer will have some men come and get 'em after he has risen from his bed and had his breakfast."

"Hammer? You don't mean Bill Hammer?"

"One and the same. You know of him?"

"I do."

"He's a decent sort, but he's long past his prime. Pretty much just a trash collector these days."

"Doesn't sound much like the man I used to know."

"He does the bidding of whoremongers and whiskey peddlers, pimps and gun artists that run this place. They might as well have him on a leash and have him sniff birds out of the bush. He's one of those old lawmen who has reached the end of the line and is just looking for a pay check. Those two dead in the street, hell, for all I know he might even have robbed their pockets, stolen their boots."

Cole recalled Bill as a good lawman at one time, tough as they came, fearless and God-fearing, always kept his nose stuck down in a Bible while eating his lunch, even on the trail. Never a preaching kind, just a quiet man who could separate the realities of life and of the commandment: "Thou shalt not kill." When one of his deputies questioned him on this commandment, he simply replied: "That means, if I was to let another man kill me, I'd be helping him to sin, now, wouldn't I? And if I kill him 'cause he don't give me no choice, well, then, I reckon the good Lord will sort it out."

But this was years ago and Cole hadn't seen the man in all that time and could only imagine what, if he was still wearing the badge, it might be like for him, especially in a place like Gun Town.

They entered through a wooden gate of a picket fence around a small nondescript house of whitewash that looked ghostly in the night. The medico unlocked a door and they entered the house. Cole followed the medico down a carpeted hall that had framed paintings on the walls and two chairs with curved arms with red upholstering as though just waiting for someone to sit in them. They looked as if no one ever had. The two men entered a small room and the medico lit a lamp that cast a yellow light, some of it falling on a metal cabinet and some on an examination table of steel.

"Sit on that table and let's have a better look at you," Pursewater said as he shucked out of his coat and rolled up the sleeves of his boiled shirt before washing his hands in a pan of water he poured from a porcelain pitcher with a large curved handle. When finished, he dried his hands on a towel, and came and stood next to Cole, drawing the lamp near.

He unwrapped the bandage, looked at the wound, and said: "Woman's under things, eh? Well, at least if you'd passed, you would have done so knowing you was wrapped in the raiment of one of God's most beauteous creatures."

"Yeah, well . . . ," Cole muttered impatiently.

"I'm going to need to débride that wound."

"You mean clean it? Don't know why you medicos have a language of your own, something us common folks can't understand."

Pursewater grunted as he set about scrubbing off the old scab and applying tincture of iodine that caused Cole to flinch from the sting.

"Now I am going to stitch you up and it might not feel too good, so I suggest we have us a taste of some good Kentucky bourbon just to steel our nerves, eh?"

He walked over to a cabinet and opened a door and took out a bottle and two metal jiggers and filled them, handing one to Cole.

"Salute," Pursewater said, and clinked his jigger with Cole's. They downed them, and Pursewater said: "Maybe it's best if you lay down, bad side up."

Cole reclined while Pursewater set to sewing closed the scalp wound with a tiny curved needle and black silk thread. Cole stood the pinch and sting until the medico was finished. He then bandaged the wound properly.

"You can sit up now."

Pursewater poured them each another jigger of the bourbon, then led Cole to a parlor with a large fireplace already stacked with firewood and kindling. Cole sat in one of two upholstered chairs, while Pursewater struck a match and set the wood to blaze, then took a seat himself.

"It's good to have someone prepare things for you," the medico said with a sigh, the tumbler in one hand, the bottle held by its neck in the other. "Got a man . . . him and his missus clean my house and prepare everything for me. Whatever would the rich do without the poor to serve them?"

"I wouldn't know," Cole said. "Hell of a whiskey, Doc."

"Help yourself to more," Pursewater said, holding forth the bottle. "This here Elijah Craig is like kissing a virgin. I have it shipped in by the case twice a year."

They drank in silence for a time. Cole could see the old boy was winding down like a $2 watch.

"I reckon I should get going," he said. "What's the fare for the repair job?"

"Aw, hell," Pursewater said, waving a hand. "Whatever you think it's worth. Just don't leave me any chickens or shoat hogs."

Cole took five silver dollars from his wallet

and laid them next to the bottle of Elijah Craig. "Where does old Bill Hammer keep himself?" he asked.

"Has an apartment up over the drugstore, down the street and across."

"Appreciate the care," Cole said, but the old boy's eyelids had already snapped shut like pulled shades.

CHAPTER FIFTEEN

Once more into the vanishing night. *Now what?* John Henry Cole asked himself. *Go home or go to hell? Good question. A regular bed with a pillow would do the trick, at least for now. Whatever needed resolving could wait, couldn't it?* Sure it could. Right after he paid a visit to an old comrade.

He walked up the street, stopping when he found the druggist's shop and climbed the stairwell that ascended the outer wall and rapped on the door with his knuckles. He waited, rapped again because he'd seen a seam of light under the door even though the hour was late.

Finally a ragged voice from within: "Go away!"

"Bill?"

"Who is it?"

"An old pal of yours, John Henry Cole."

More silence, then the door opened a crack and a haggard, gray-bearded face with squinted eyes under shaggy brows peered out, a lamp held near.

"Who'd you say?"

"John Henry Cole, you remember me?"

"Cole's dead," he said, and started to close the door.

"No, Bill, I'm not dead. I'm standing right here."

187

The door opened a bit wider and the old man brought the lamp nearer Cole's face. Bill Hammer had filled out from the whipsaw-thin man he had once been. Now there was paunch and thick chest and freckled hands.

"Shit," he said at last. "What you doin' here, John Henry?"

"It's a long story. But I heard you were the lawdog in town and thought I'd drop by and see how you were faring?"

Bill Hammer stepped aside to admit Cole into the apartment of two small rooms sparsely furnished with a narrow bed over in one corner, two chairs, and an upholstered footstool with fringe.

Bill Hammer set the lamp down and then himself into one of the two chairs. He was in his nightshirt, the whitish hair on his head sticking up like the feathers of a pullet. Cole sat opposite.

"This is what it's come to, John Henry," Bill said, looking about him apologetically. "A fellow works hard his whole life, tries to do the right thing . . . doesn't always, but tries . . . and he ends up living like some broken-dick store clerk just waiting for death like a fellow waiting for the midnight cannonball."

"Lots I've known have ended up worse," Cole said.

"Yeah, but that ain't exactly a comfort, knowing others had it worse than you, knowing others is younger, no more so than others is vital and still got their whole lives ahead of them yet."

"How'd you end up here in Gun Town?"

The older man's hoary eyebrows knitted and his brow furrowed either from trying to remember or trying to forget. "It was Lucky Jack," Bill said. "He come across me last year in Bozeman, seen how I was, took pity on me, and said he could get me the job here if I wanted it. 'Course I wanted it! I told him. It beat hell out of swamping out saloons in Bozeman, sleeping in a horse stall."

"Yes, sir, I can see where it would."

"You want a drink or something?"

"Could use a smoke."

Bill Hammer raised up out of his chair and went into the far room—the one with a narrow bed—and returned and handed Cole his makings. He watched Cole work with deft fingers to construct a cigarette, then struck a match and held the flame to the end of the cigarette and waited until Cole drew in a lungful of smoke and exhaled it again.

"Damn, you know how often I quit the habit?" Cole said.

"Probably about the same as all of us have. It's a hard habit to break. That and chewing is."

"I quit every time I put one out," Cole said.

The lawman reached for the tobacco and papers and built himself one and said: "Me, too."

"Jeanne?" Cole said as Bill Hammer licked the

edge of the paper before twisting off the ends of his cigarette.

"Dead," Bill said, striking a match. "Yours?"

"Also dead. My little boy, too."

"Damn' shame, ain't it? The good ones should die and us 'uns should yet live with all our sins."

"It is. But I got lucky, too."

"How so?"

"Learned I had another son recently. A boy grown into a man. His name is Tom Moon."

Bill exhaled a thick cloud of smoke. "Well, that's something. He along with you?"

Cole explained about Tom's being the marshal in Red Pony.

"Followed in your footsteps, then?"

"Didn't want him to."

"Nothing wrong with doing the law."

"No, sir."

"What happened to your noggin, you got that bandage around it?"

Cole told him the story, keeping it brief as he could.

"I hate a back-shooter almost as bad as I do a horse thief," he said. "What's this damn' world coming to? You try and help a feller and he back-shoots you?"

"Don't know."

"No damn' good, is what. Folks ain't got no morals no more."

Cole attributed much of what the old man was

saying to the words of everyone who lived long enough and witnessed first hand the changes in a society. He simply nodded in agreement.

"Don't reckon you got a bottle on you?" Bill Hammer said. "I drunk up the last drop of what I got in the house."

"No, sir."

"Damn' pity."

"You used to be a hard-shell Baptist as I recall," Cole said.

"Used to be a lot of things I ain't no more. Got to where what I'd read in the Good Book made less and less sense the older I got. I figured the devil had blinded my eyes to the words, so I set it aside. How come you ain't dead?"

"Pardon?"

"I heard three or four times you was killed, over in the Nations, in Kansas . . . that you got wiped out with Custer whilst you guided him. All sorts of stories."

Cole smiled. "Well, I guess like someone once said . . . the story of my demise has been greatly exaggerated."

"Who was it said that?"

"I don't know."

"So, considering everything what's gone on, you still intend to see the job of getting this woman back from Lucky Jack, seeing how the sons don't seem to want her back and the old man is dying?"

"I don't know," Cole admitted. "I'm thinking about just going home."

"Probably be best if you did, son. Nothing here for a man like you except trouble."

"You work for him?"

Bill Hammer took a long time before answering, seemingly lost in the pleasure of smoking his cigarette, then said softly: "I work for all of 'em. The bar owners and whoremongers are the ones what pay my wages. I do the best I can to maintain some sense of order, but look around," he said with a sweep of his arm as if all could be seen from his room. "The only real order in this town is that there ain't any. My hope these days is to die peaceful in my bed, not shot through the lungs, coughing up blood. I pay my rent and buy my meals and send a little home to my daughter Minnie, 'cause she's got three youngsters and no husband. You remember Minnie?"

"Somewhat," Cole said.

"I'd advise you to get on the next flyer and leave this place, leave all this business of Lucky Jack and the woman behind you. You can't win that fight, son. You want to fight something, go and fight what you can win. Now, if you don't mind, I'd like to go back to bed, my bones is tired."

Cole shook his old friend's hand, noted the trembling that comes from age and not from fear, and bid him a good night. The door closed behind him with a soft, almost pathetic click as if Bill Hammer was locking out John Henry Cole and the rest of the town's troubles.

He walked to the hotel and bought a room and went into it and undressed down to his skin and eased onto the bed, letting weariness drag him under. He fell into a restless sleep, and when he next became aware, the dawn was spreading over the land like dirty gray water sloshed from a bucket.

CHAPTER SIXTEEN

"You'll never guess who's in town?" Gypsy Flynn said.

It was midmorning and Lucky Jack was just getting dressed in a fine coat of black broadcloth over a freshly starched white shirt with a paper collar, his striped trousers tucked down into polished boots.

"You look like a politician," Lenora had said just before Gypsy came barging in. She quickly covered herself as she sat propped up in bed, her hair unpinned and cascading down to her shoulders.

"Don't you ever knock, damn it!"

Gypsy looked at her with those feral eyes, looked at her as if he knew the secret she had to keep from Lucky lest he pitch her out, lest he put a bullet in her brain or both their brains. It was a dangerous secret to be sure, but one he seemed to relish nonetheless.

Lucky Jack was standing in front of the full-length mirror, appraising himself, and did not turn to respond to Gypsy's question, but simply said: "Who?"

Gypsy was standing there, his creased and sweat-stained Stetson pulled down so tightly it bent his ears over and covered up the scalped sides of his bowl haircut that made him look like the cold killer he was. He seemed almost to tremble with the news he was about to deliver.

"John Henry Cole!"

Now Lucky Jack *did* turn.

"John Henry? Can't be. He got himself killed in Tahlequah."

"Well, if so, he's done riz from the grave. Got himself a room over at the hotel."

"How do you know?"

"How else, but ol' Bill Hammer. John Henry come to see him last evening, was saying how he ended up here accidental after being back-shot. Said he also talked about being hired by her husband." Gypsy pointed with his nose toward Lenora. "Guess you know now who Wilson sent. Whether or not he brung the cash is a different story."

Lucky considered the news for a moment. It seemed a strange twist of fate that he would encounter John Henry Cole in such a manner after all these years. The fact was, he liked and admired Cole in spite of Cole's honesty and devotion to a life that led nowhere.

"You sure about this? Wasn't just that old drunk's mind playing tricks on him like it sometimes does?" Lucky asked, putting a brace of silver pearl-handled pistols into the scarlet sash he wrapped around his waist—something he'd once seen Wild Bill Hickok affecting and he had always admired the style.

"He sure enough sounded like he knew what he was talking about. Said he wanted to warn you of John Henry's existence in order to avoid a blood bath. Said he hoped you two could work out your differences, but also said John Henry was thinking of quitting the game anyway since the boy who shot him was Wilson's kid."

Lenora knew without the name being spoken who had shot this John Henry Cole—Bo Wilson. He was the only one with the temperament to back-shoot a man.

"Well, I'm a son-of-a-bitch," Lucky Jack said, more to himself than the others as he adjusted the revolvers butt forward, then admired his overall appearance.

"Who's John Henry Cole?" Lenora said.

"An old law pard' of mine back in the day when we was honest men wearing deputy marshal badges. Only man I know who could best him in a fight is me," Lucky Jack said confidently.

"I'd like to see that . . . you and him gunning it out," Gypsy said, thinking it would be wonderful if the two killed each other, then it would just be him running things and Lenora could like it or else.

"Well, maybe I should go and pay him a visit."

"I reckon was it me, I would," Gypsy said.

"Let him know he's not welcome and, if he don't like it, put a couple of hot slugs in him for entertainment."

The two of them studied each other for a moment, the room fragrant with Lenora's French perfume and cigar smoke and whiskey still in glasses on the bedside stand.

"Please, no more killing," she said.

Gypsy sort of smiled that wicked smile of his. "My knife went into that Pinkerton's liver like soft butter. But I'm not the only one who's gonna get my hands bloody."

"Shut up!" Lucky said.

"I'd like to get dressed now," Lenora said.

"Come on," Lucky said to Gypsy. "Let's go say hidey-ho to my old pal."

Lenora exhaled when the two of them left the room. She climbed out of bed in her altogether and locked the door, then washed herself as best she could from the basin, and quickly dressed. She didn't know why exactly she felt panicky, she just did. She needed to get out of the room and go somewhere and do something other than be where she was and what she was.

Over at the hotel in a room not much larger than a jail cell and no better furnished, Cole had already risen and dressed. He still had a bottle of the cure-all he'd found in his coat pocket and swallowed the last of it, then went in search of something he felt badly that he needed.

He descended the stairs and crossed the lobby, pausing only long enough to ask the clerk if there was a gunsmith in town.

"Up the street and around the first corner," the clerk directed. "The Jew, Adelmann. Can make a gun out of a length of pig iron."

Abe Adelmann was repairing a Colt .45 Peacemaker with a broken firing pin when Cole entered his gun shop.

Abe peered over the rims of his spectacles. "How might I help you?"

Cole glanced at the rack of long guns on the wall behind the counter. "Need something wicked mean."

"You mean besides that hogleg you're wearing in that shoulder rig?"

"A lot meaner."

"Meanest I got are those two shotguns," the gunsmith said, half turning toward the rack.

"That coach gun. What gauge is it?"

The gunsmith reached for the double-barrel coach gun. "Remington, twenty inch barrels, ten gauge of double meanness. Cut a man right directly in half you hit him full on at his belt buckle." He handed the gun to Cole.

Cole hefted it, broke it open.

"Rabbit-ear hammers," the gunsmith added. "Bought it off a broke dick cowboy last month used to hire on sometimes as a stagecoach messenger, or so he claimed. Hell, for all I know, he might have robbed it off a stage."

Abe Adelmann, was a thin man with pencil-thin mustaches and eyes as clear blue as glass marbles that peered out with intensity behind his wire-rimmed spectacles.

"How much?" Cole asked.

"Thirty dollars and worth more."

"It's a deal."

"Here's a box of shells to go with it. You need any for that hogleg?"

"I'm good."

There was an entire glass case full of handguns with tags hanging from strings tied around the trigger guards. The air in the shop smelled of gun oil and metal shavings.

Cole came out, carrying the coach gun in one hand by the forestock, both barrels loaded, his coat pocket heavy with extra shells.

He went up the street until he found a mercantile and went in and bought a new Stetson hat to replace the lost one and to cover his bandaged head, a sack of Bull Durham, rolling papers, and matches. He felt a lot better.

He went up the street to the end of town where the train station stood alongside twin ribbons of steel track that gleamed dully in the sun, the air scented with cinder and creosote, and went inside the office.

A bald-headed man, wearing a green visor

that looked like a duck's bill, peered at Cole as he entered the small square room full of warm light and dust motes. The sun's heat brought out the mustiness of dry floorboards and bare-wood walls.

"When's the next flyer east?" Cole asked.

"Due in at midnight," the station manager said.

"How much for a ticket to Red Pony?"

"I'll have to look it up. Red Pony, you say?"

Cole nodded.

The station manager flipped through a book with towns and schedules till he found Red Pony by way of Cisco and then Two Rivers and later Gentile and on into Mason before it stopped in Red Pony.

"Twenty-three dollars," the manager said, "all told. Be about fifteen hours to get you there."

"I'll take a ticket then."

The manager made out a ticket, passed it through the window bars, and took Cole's money. "Good enough."

"Where's the telegraph office?"

The station man told him, and Cole stepped outside again. He'd hoped that he could clear town and get back home before anything happened, if it was to happen. He had a bad feeling about Woman being there alone and not knowing what that crazy bastard, Bo Wilson, might try.

He made his way back up the street to the telegrapher's, a small shop squeezed in between a boot maker's and dentist's office, and went in. The telegrapher was a man with bony wrists and narrow-set eyes and looked like he'd been there his whole life. He was eating a pickle and reading a dime novel about Buffalo Bill raising the first scalp for Custer, and set both book and pickle aside when Cole handed him a message to send to Tom in Red Pony.

Tom. Need you to go and gather Woman. STOP. Take her to town and keep watch over her until I get back. STOP. Returning soon. STOP. JHC.

"Send it now," Cole said.

The telegrapher charged him $1 and Cole gladly paid it, then took his leave.

Now I need a cup of hot coffee, he thought, and went up the street to the German's café. Surprisingly it was empty. Cole grabbed a table by the window and a skinny man in an apron came over and said: "What'll it be, bub?"

"Coffee, fried eggs, and hash."

"That it?"

"Where's the German lady?"

"She runs the graveyard shift. I handle the days. She likes to palaver with the drunks and whores and I hate them . . . the whole dirty bunch."

The skinny man was taller than Cole, handsome but for a whitish left eye that looked like a teaspoon of milk. He went back to the kitchen, returned with a pot of coffee and a cup, and set them both down. "Help yourself, bub," he said, and went back to the kitchen.

Cole laid the coach gun atop the table and poured himself a cup of the Arbuckle's, and then built a cigarette and lit it, drew in a lungful of smoke and exhaled it. Sipped the coffee. It was surprisingly good. Life seemed a tad better even though his head was still sore as a smashed thumb.

The skinny man returned and set down a plate with hash and two eggs sunny-side-up, then wiped his hands on his long apron.

"Surprised you're not busier at this hour," Cole said.

The man shrugged. "Breakfast crowd's all come and gone already. The whores and pimps and gamblers sleep late and won't come in till noon for their breakfast. It's what I call the waning hour. You mind I sit and have a smoke with you while you eat?"

"No, I don't mind."

The man sat, made himself a cigarette, and borrowed a match from Cole to light it. It was a poorly made cigarette, too loosely wound and too fat. The paper burned and sizzled at the touch of the match and the man looked down his nose at it, the milk eye quivering.

"Haven't seen the likes of you around before,"

the man said, idly staring out the window, watching his exhaled smoke curl up against the fly-specked glass.

"That a question?" Cole said, cutting into his eggs.

"No, just an observation. Don't see many men walking around with shotguns these days, casual-like."

"Another question?"

"No, just an observation."

The eggs were the best Cole had ever tasted.

"Cook 'em in butter," the man said proudly when he saw the satisfied look on Cole's face. "That's the secret to most things. Learned that from a Frenchman who was a deserter from the Foreign Legion. Said he used to cook for rich people before he joined. Them damn' French! Name's Peck, by the way." He extended a hand.

Cole shook it, then concentrated on his breakfast. It seemed that everybody he ran into had a story to tell.

"You should be aware that this is the sort of place where men who go about openly with guns often shoot one another," Peck said.

"Another observation?"

"Somebody shot two men last night. Found their bodies right out there on the street. Sheriff Hammer just had them hauled off to the bone orchard like dead steers."

"Common occurrence, is it?"

"Mighty common. They'll kill you over nothing in this town . . . over a dime or your shirt. Christ, I never seen no place like this."

"How come you stay?"

The fellow's fingers were stained yellow from too many cigarettes. Cole guessed him to be not more than thirty, coal black hair, his good eye deep blue with a touch of worry. "Hell if I know," he said, drawing on his shuck. "Thought I wanted to be a cowboy. Came from back East . . . New York, where I was a student of the law. Read too many of those damn' dime novels, got itchy feet. Now here I sit, frying eggs like a Frenchman and wishing I was anywhere but here."

"Could always leave, couldn't you?"

"Could, but not sure where I'd go. Just waiting for the muse to strike."

"Muse?"

"I believe in fate, in whispers from the muse."

"Jesus," Cole said, and scraped up some more eggs and washed them down with coffee. "Bill Hammer doesn't do anything about it . . . the random killing?"

"Bill Hammer is morally a righteous old fellow, but he ain't no sort of real lawman. Does what they tell him to do. No more, no less."

Cole felt badly for his old friend, but he understood how it could be, too. "Well, I'll be on my caution," he said, patting the thick metal breech of the coach gun with its Adams Company Express engraved in the side plate.

Cole continued to eat and Peck smoked, his legs crossed at the knee. Then suddenly Peck said—"Oh, oh."—as he gazed out the window.

"What is it?"

"Trouble's on the prod."

Cole looked out the window in the direction the cook was staring, his good eye agleam like a wet stone. Lucky Jack and Gypsy Flynn were coming up the walk, Lucky with his confident stride and Gypsy gimping beside him, both looking for all the world like men out for a killing. Lucky with those twin butts of his revolvers facing forward, Flynn limping alongside with his eyes cast downward.

The door rattled open and in they came. Their eyes met those of Cole and the cook's, and held level until Lucky Jack smiled a broad smile that was more sinister than joyful. He came over, The Gimp shuffling behind him.

"I heard you was in town," Lucky Jack said, extending his hand to Cole. The cook scooted his chair back in order to head for the kitchen.

Cole did not take Lucky's hand, and Lucky let it fall by his side as his gaze fell to the coach gun on the table. "I heard you'd gotten yourself slain in Tahlequah some years back," Lucky Jack said, taking up the seat vacated by the cook.

"If I didn't know better, I'd say I was killed,

too, listening to everybody tell me I was dead. But as we can both see, I'm pretty much alive."

"Obviously," Lucky Jack said, removing his fine dove-gray Stetson hat and laying it, brim up, on the table next to the shotgun. "Never knew you to carry a scatter-gun, John Henry. Those things are usually for old men and the blind."

"I guess you'll have to judge for yourself if I'm either one." Cole eyed the other man, The Gimp, saw that he was armed with revolvers in crossed holsters that rode high on his hips. It looked like a lot of weight for such a banty-size man. If he tumbled accidentally into a river, all that weight would drag him under. "You look like a banker," he said to Lucky Jack. "That, or a pimp."

The smile remained on Lucky Jack's face but it was tight as a newly strung wire. "Well, let's just say I've had a successful streak of luck. What you doing here?"

"Eating breakfast. Waiting for the train."

There was a moment of silence between them. The Gimp looked ready to spring. Cole was almost hoping that he would. He didn't like the man even though he didn't know a thing about him.

"That so?" Lucky Jack said acidly. "How is it you come to Gun Town just to eat breakfast and catch a train, is what I'm asking."

"I know what you're asking and it's none of your damned business."

"I tend to disagree with you," Lucky said. "But, you see, whatever goes on in this town *is* my business."

Cole took out his makings and slowly built himself a cigarette, even though he had no desire to smoke it. The best thing he could do was just wait for the midnight flyer and get on, go home to Woman, and to hell with the rest of it. But he didn't care to be prodded by Lucky Jack Dancer or anybody else. And that's what it felt like— Lucky Jack was prodding him. "I was shot, my horse run off," Cole said, pausing briefly to point to his bandaged head. "As it happened, this was the nearest town. Now you know."

"You always had a string of luck, John Henry," Lucky replied, then called to the cook to bring some extra cups, which the man did, then quickly retreated again.

For a moment Lucky Jack sipped his coffee and watched Cole as he lit his smoke. Then he said: "Well, now, ain't that the oddest coincidence . . . you showing up on my home turf, after all these years. I mean, what are the chances you'd get shot so close to here?"

"I reckon maybe it is kind of strange."

"I heard about you, Cole," The Gimp said, standing off a few feet. The Gimp's voice was like a door opening on rusted hinges. He had them sharp little rat's teeth and a shaggy mustache that looked like it belonged on a sheepdog.

Cole took him all in now—the slouching stance, the hooded eyes, the nervous tic in his jaw muscle, the sheathed knife. Cole had seen his likes before, the sort who would slit your throat while you slept. "You're Gypsy Flynn, the one called The Gimp," Cole said, and saw the way the recognition caused the man to flinch, surprised a man like Cole would know his name.

"Nobody calls me that," he said.

"I guess we've heard of each other," Cole said calmly, his hands steady, purposeful.

"Go get yourself some breakfast," Lucky Jack said. "Let me and my old friend palaver a bit."

Flynn hesitated a beat, then went to another corner of the room and took a seat facing them.

"The Gimp can be a caution," Lucky said. "Best not to rile him too much. He has a firecracker temper."

Lucky had put on bulk, his jowls heavy, his face more brooding. And though he wore those fine clothes and his hair was pomaded, and the pinky ring with a blood red ruby set in gold flashed when he poured himself a cup of the Arbuckle's, he was still a killer of the first rank.

"What is it you need, Lucky?" Cole asked.

"Who says I need anything?"

"Let's cut the crap," Cole said. "Bill Hammer let you know I was in town and he told you what I told him, about being hired by Wilson. It was Wilson's boy who shot me because he didn't want his stepmother back. The bullet fired from his gun changed my contract far as I'm concerned. You've got Wilson's wife, we both know it, so what's your play?"

"My play? Ha. John Henry, the only reason I can think for you to be here is to try and kill me, regardless of that lame story about your contract being finished. I never knew you *not* to finish a job, regardless."

Cole thought about this a moment and then said: "No, it was never my plan to kill you. The plan was simply to get the woman back. I figured a man of your abilities would see that, take the money, and let bygones be bygones."

"Men like us never negotiate when we know we don't have to, John Henry."

"Only if that's how you want to play it."

Lucky Jack's smile came on slow as a sunset. "You know I've got a lot of reward money on my head. Maybe you foresaw a whole lot more at stake here than just what Wilson was paying you."

"Then you'd best be cautious about Pinkertons." Cole said it purposely to see Lucky's reaction, and he saw it in the tic just under the eye—the tic that always jerked whenever Lucky got himself ready for a fight.

"Shit, Pinkertons and any other laws best stay clear of Gun Town if they know what's good for them. Ask the last one who came here."

"I would, but he's dead."

"God damn right he is," Lucky said almost mockingly.

"You need to send that woman back to her husband."

"Says who?"

"It's the decent thing to do. Her husband is dying."

Lucky leaned back in his chair, his clear-eyed gaze without a hint of what he was thinking. "I thought you said your contract was null and void with that man?"

"I said shooting me changed the contract. I didn't say anything about it being null and void."

"So then you *did* come to get the woman, after all."

"Just let it go, Lucky. You and me have no quarrel."

"She goes back when that old fool sends me five thousand dollars."

"He's already sent you the money."

"Like hell. That Pinkerton tried to play me. He didn't have any damn' money with him."

"Then somebody lied to you, but it wasn't Wilson."

"Well, either it's your affair or it ain't, which is it, John Henry?"

"I've said my piece. I'm headed home on the midnight flyer."

"That's it, then?"

"That's it."

Lucky Jack leaned forward, leaned in close, conspiratorially, and said in a hushed voice: "I could really use a man like you, John Henry. A real business partner, somebody I could trust . . . like in the old days in the Nations. A pair of aces like us could live high and have a damn' lot of fun doing it . . . die happy in our beds between the best-looking whores in all the United States!"

Cole glanced toward Flynn who was staring bullet holes into him. "What about The Gimp? You just going to leave him out in the cold, put me in his place?"

Lucky glanced around at Gypsy Flynn, then back at Cole. "He's a god-damn' assassin, that's all he is. He's my bulldog, does what I tell him, but he ain't nothing more than that. I can hire all the assassins like him I want. To hell with him if you want in. I'll kill him myself just to prove it to you. Just say the word and I'll kill him now, on the spot, graveyard dead."

"It's mighty tempting to see him stiff and growing cold, Lucky. But I've got other plans."

"Such as?"

"Like I said . . . going home."

"Think about it," Lucky said. "I keep a place over the Liberty just up the street. You want to see me, just ask at the bar."

Lucky stood, and when he did, so did Gypsy

Flynn. Cole glanced The Gimp's way again. "You're right, Lucky. He's your dog."

Lucky laughed and motioned for Gypsy to follow him out. Cole breathed a sigh of relief for he had thought he might have to kill Lucky and The Gimp and probably get killed in doing it.

"Hey!" he called. The cook peeked out from the kitchen. "How about some more of that coffee and a piece of pie, if there is any?"

When the cook brought him the coffee and pie, he said: "What the hell did you say your name was?"

"Peck." Then, looking at the recently closed door, Lucky's hair-oil scent still lingering, he added: "But some like him calls me Pecker."

"Mister Peck, have you seen a woman with Lucky lately? A refined woman?"

The cook looked up and out the window and said indirectly: "Yeah, a real good-looking one, too, not the usual whores Lucky's known to solicit."

"She stay there where he does, up over the Liberty saloon?"

"Keeps her there on a pretty short leash."

Cole nodded, dug into his pie with his fork, and plopped it in his mouth and chewed. Then he asked, "What sort of pie is this?"

"Huckleberry."

"I thought so. I ain't had a piece of huckleberry since I was a kid."

"How's it taste?"

"You made it?"

"No, Gerta makes 'em nights in between the drunks and whores."

"Damned good pie."

"You aiming to tangle with ol' Lucky and that little assassin of his?" Peck said, glancing at the coach gun. "Ain't many would miss them two and their bunch in this town."

"How many they got in their bunch?"

"Seven, eight, any given time. They come and go, so the number keeps changing."

"No, I'm not aiming to tangle with them. I'm just a man what got shot off his horse and landed here and is trying to get back home again."

Peck eyed him more carefully now. "You ever was in Bozeman?"

"Yeah," Cole said, taking a second bite of pie.

"What'd you do in Bozeman?"

"That's a lot of questions."

"I'm nosy."

"You ought not to be. It could land you in trouble with some men."

"I know it, but I can't help my curiosity."

"I kept around Bozeman for a time. Was on the police commission for a while, but not overly long."

"Thought so. You probably don't recall but you arrested me once."

"Small world," Cole said, eating more of the

pie and washing it down with more of the coffee.

"You didn't buffalo or abuse me none like some of them deputies used to."

"Not my way of doing things."

"I always figured I was ever to get arrested again, I'd want it to be in Bozeman."

Cole half smiled. "I'd not recommend it. What'd I arrest you for?"

"Drunk and loitering."

"Yeah, they're not much keen on drunk and loitering in Bozeman."

"You told the judge there wasn't a man in this world that wouldn't sometimes get down on his luck. Got him to suspend sentencing and you walked me down to the train station and bought me a ticket out of town."

"Sorry I don't remember it. Looks like it turned out all right."

The waiter nodded. "I could've ended up worse, I suppose. Gerta took me on 'cause I could cook, and it turned out OK."

"Good for you. What's the fare?" Cole stood away from the table, leaving behind an empty cup and a scraped plate of huckleberry smear.

"On the house, for what you did."

"Not necessary," Cole said, reaching for his wallet.

"No, no, it *is*."

"Thank you kindly."

They shook hands, and Cole went out, a lit

cigarette dangling from his lip, and stood for a time on the boardwalk looking up and down the street of Gun Town, thinking about Woman. He watched a pair of riders on high-stepping horses come up the street, men in suits and bowler hats, their mounts thoroughbreds tossing their heads and chewing the iron bits in their mouths. A cur dog trotted after them like it was curious as to where they were going.

It would be ten hours yet before the flyer arrived, and it seemed like too much time to kill. And too much time to kill always left a lot of time for a man to do his thinking, as Cole did as he crossed the street and took up residence down the way, across from Karl's Liberty Palace Saloon, on a chair out front of a barbershop with its red and white striped barber pole. As he sat there, he thought: *I never quit a job before it was finished and I wonder why I'm considering quitting it now, regardless of the circumstances? It wasn't Wilson who shot me. It was Bo. And it was with the father I made the bargain, not with the son. The old man is dying and it would be his wish to see his wife again, if I could bring her to him. I know it would be mine.*

A teamster went down the street, cursing his mules and cracking his whip over their flicking ears, the wagon rocking to and fro nearly losing its canvas-covered load and scattering pedestrians like chickens. A man crossing the street barely got clear of the onrushing freight, and he turned and cursed the driver who only bellowed and cursed back with a great deal of delight.

No sir, I'd be a quitter and a thief if I was to take Wilson's money and not see the job done. And, besides, I've still got many hours to wait and what the hell else would I do but kill time? He felt relieved at having put a certainty to his thoughts, even as another voice popped up and argued: *You'd be a damned fool to concern yourself further with this business. Why do it?* The first voice said: *Because . . .* The other voice said: *Aw, hell.*

Cole finished his shuck, flipped it away, and waited. He wanted to see Wilson's wife—either by chance if she emerged from the saloon, or by going in to find her.

The shotgun lay across his knees, a comfort to him.

CHAPTER SEVENTEEN

Woman saw a rider coming. She had the eyes of an eagle, and although the rider was still a great distance away and had not yet formed into a recognizable man, she believed that it was John Henry Cole returning. She could tell by the way he rode a horse, as if rider and horse were all one thing, the rider an extension of the horse and the horse an extension of the rider.

She stood in the doorway, hopeful, glad to see him returning, for she'd had several bad dreams about him since he'd left with those men who'd hired him, had paid him all that money. Nobody pays so much money for a job easily done, one without danger. But Cole had insisted that they needed the money to achieve their aims and she had not argued with him for it was not her way to try and change a man's mind.

She had just finished eating her breakfast and the sky was bright and clean as a freshly washed blue shirt, the air yet cool, the sun not yet having reached its zenith. She watched the rider come on in a fine golden dust for he came from the east, the town of Red Pony, and the sun was to his back, causing the dust to glow. There was something spiritual in watching the rider coming, surrounded as if by a halo, as if the Great Spirit had appointed him to come. Her heart quickened until the rider grew near enough for her to see that it wasn't Cole at all, but his son Tom, the marshal of Red Pony. Tom had that long black hair of his mother's people, but the chiseled facial features of Cole, the same unflinching gaze. Her chest tightened for she feared that the only reason Tom would come to see her was to tell her bad news about Cole. Something had happened.

He rode into the yard, the chickens protesting and scattering like angry biddies. Tom's bay horse was sweated, which meant he'd ridden it hard. The ride to Red Pony in an easy lope would take an hour over the eastbound road. By wagon two or three.

Tom drew reins and dismounted, not in a rush, but more calmly than a man who might be delivering bad news.

"Woman," he said.

"Tom."

They barely knew each other for the relationship between her and Cole was barely three months along and she'd only been introduced to Tom once when she and Cole had purposely ridden into town together in the buckboard to get supplies and eat at the restaurant there, as if Cole had wanted to show her off to everyone and anyone. He'd taken the occasion to introduce her then to Tom who seemed almost reluctant to be introduced.

Cole had explained already to her about his relationship with Tom, how the two of them had only recently reunited as father and son, how Cole had not even known he'd had a son until he learned it from Tom's mother. The one thing that she and Tom shared was their Indian blood and it was bond enough even if nothing else figured into it. So now here he was, having ridden his horse hard, and for what purpose, to what end, she wondered.

"I got a wire from my father," Tom said. "He wants you to come with me into town."

"Cole come?" she said.

"No. He wants you to come with me," Tom said, gesturing to help with the language barrier between them.

"Why come?" she said.

"He's OK. You understand? John Henry's OK. But he wants you to come with me into town, into Red Pony."

She shook her head. "No."

Tom repeated Cole's request, tapping the piece of paper in his hands. She knew the words written on the paper came over the wire that the Indians called "singing" but how it did was a mystery.

"I wait for him," she said. "Here."

"Shit," he said in frustration.

"Eat?" she said.

"Sure, why not, maybe a little time to think about how I can change your mind."

She brought him fry bread and beans and some cured bear meat and strong black Arbuckle's coffee and watched him eat there on the porch, looking off in the distance as if watchful for Cole himself.

Tom didn't know what to say to her but—"Thank you."—when he handed her back the plate. "You sure you won't come with me?"

"I stay here, wait for him," she repeated.

"I reckon," he said, and led his horse to the water trough and waited for it to drink, then mounted and said: "I'll come in a few days and check on you, see if you've changed your mind. I'll let John Henry know you wouldn't come with me."

She simply looked at him with the nearly black, wet-stone eyes, and though she was not beautiful, Tom could see how his father would be attracted to her, for she lent a presence of strength not common in most women, one of loyalty as well. She had strong fine-boned features and was handsome in her darkness of skin.

He nodded, then turned the bay out toward the road, and she watched him go just as he'd come, in a haze of dust rising and settling back to earth behind him. At least Cole was not dead, she told herself.

It was not two days more when she saw another rider approaching down the same road and again she thought at first it might be Cole, guessed it would be, but as the shape of rider and horse grew more recognizable she could see that it was neither Cole nor Tom, but a man who rode a horse altogether differently, who rode more stiffly in the saddle and seemed to be a separate entity to the horse. She stood just in the doorway, within easy reach of the rifle kept on the inside wall.

It was not until the man was within a dozen yards of the house that she saw that it was one of the men who'd hired Cole, the one in age between the old one and the young one.

He rode up and, without asking, dismounted and came forward, still holding the reins in his hand.

"Ma'am," he said, tipping his hat. Her fingers nearly touched the rifle's forestock—a repeating rifle fully loaded with sixteen cartridges.

"It's your husband, ma'am," the fellow said. "He's been hurt, shot. You understand?"

She simply stared at him until the man made a gesture with his hand, forming it into a gun shape and pointing it at himself, pretending to pull the trigger, then staggering exaggeratedly around in the yard.

"Shot!" he repeated, and pointed at her. "Your husband's been shot!"

She felt the fear rise in her.

"Come! I'll take you to him. Hurry."

He motioned for her to come.

She rushed off the porch to him and said: "Cole? He shoot?"

That's when the fellow, quick as a snake, grabbed her up, one arm around her waist and the other across her chest and dragged her to the house, saying only one word: "Bitch!"

He pulled her inside and kicked the door shut, and she fought him as best as she could, but he was strong. His arms were like steel bands around her.

"Where's the money my father gave you?" he demanded. She screamed and tried clawing his face, but he twisted her hard and nearly snapped her neck, and the pain shot down through her spine causing her temporarily to go limp. Then he let loose of her and backhanded her across the face, knocking her to the floor.

"Where's the damn' money?" he shouted as if she could not hear. She'd clamped her hand to the split lip the blow had created, blood trickling through her fingers, her eyes fierce, resentful, full of hatred.

"I will god damn' kill you if you don't give me the money!"

The money meant nothing to her, and she knew what he was asking for, but the fact that he'd struck her was more than enough reason to refuse him what he wanted. She was already planning on how she could kill him—a knife in the kitchen, the rifle if she could reach it, a chunk of firewood by the stove.

He removed his belt and doubled it around his fist, buckle end hanging loose, and began to whip her with it, the metal buckle biting into her flesh and tearing at her clothing, each blow more powerful it seemed than the previous one. She could not help but cry out against the pain, and the more she cried out, the harder he swung. And the harder he swung the more flesh was torn, the more blood, the more pain until her entire body felt aflame.

"Give me the money!" he kept shouting at her as he swung the belt down on her. She'd curled up into a ball with her bloody hands covering her face and head as best they could. So he whipped her across the legs and buttocks, the effort of the beating causing him to labor, so intense had it become.

She did her best to kick him away, but it was like trying to swat flies. She'd retreated into a corner but it was the perfect place to take a beating because there was no escaping.

Finally he ran out of steam and stood bent over, hands on knees and breathing hard, the buckle clinking against the floorboards as he held the belt limply in his hand like a dead snake. He found a chair and pulled it over and sat in it, facing her.

"You stupid, stupid bitch," he said, breathing

hard. "Instead of just giving me the money, you take a beating. What the hell is wrong with your kind, anyway?"

She lay huddled up, not saying a word, afraid that if she did, it would incite him more. Every inch of her burned with the pain and she felt the wetness of blood in several places.

For several minutes they were like that, victim and villain, until he stood at last and came over and grabbed her by the hair and dragged her across the room to the off room that was her and Cole's bedroom. Lifting her by the hair, he slapped her face and threw her back on the bed, saying: "This is where you do it with him, huh. Take off your clothes."

She did not move.

He took out a large clasp knife and opened the blade and showed it to her.

"You ever had a man cut you?"

She forced herself to show no fear of him even though inside she was trembling.

"I mean cut you where it really matters?"

Silence.

She was dressed in a long loose skirt and blouse that morning for she'd planned on inside work. She had *huaraches* on her feet. He leaned over her and used the knife blade to slice open the front of her peasant blouse, exposing her breasts that were now welted and stung with pain from the beating.

"You want to take off your clothes or you want me to finish cutting them off?"

Although she could not understand the words exactly, she knew the meaning of what he was saying. She did not move, but wished he would give her a chance to get hold of the knife. So young and so cruel, she thought. Just a boy with a man's viciousness to him. He touched the knife tip to her chest, pressed enough to spark a fresh jewel of blood. She said to him—"Kill me!"—but he did not understand.

Instead, he cut open her skirt and looked upon her nakedness with a hard glint in his eyes. "Don't you move," he commanded as he started to unbutton his trousers. She kicked at him in that brief moment of letting his guard down, kicked where it hurt a man, and with this momentary distraction she leaped from the bed and ran toward the door and the rifle beside it, got her hands on it, and was bringing it around when he hit her with a clubbing blow of his fist, stunning her so completely that the rifle clattered from her hands to the floor.

"You want to shoot me!" he screamed. "You damn' heathen bitch!"

He kicked her several times as she lay on the floor. Each kick cracked ribs and shot new pain into her chest.

"I'm going to find that money," he seethed, "right after I take care of you."

Once more he dragged her by the hair toward the bedroom, this time her body limp. He picked her up and threw her on the bed and finished what he'd begun before she'd driven a heel into him.

He had no lust for her. It was purely a matter of revenge upon her for resisting him, for not doing what he'd told her to do. She lay only half conscious as he worked over her, his face a smear in her blurred vision, for her eyes had begun to swell shut from the beating and her head swam so that she only half realized what was happening to her. The fire of pain consumed her.

It was over quickly and she felt his weight come off of her and then she was alone. She could not tell if he'd left the room or not. She heard the closing of the door, a chair scrape, things being knocked over in the other rooms. In a brief moment of clarity she thought: *He will find the box of money, and when he does he will leave me alone, and then things will be over and Cole will come home again and everything will be all right.*

It was not until the smoke came in under the door and she could hear the crackling of wood and began to cough that she sat up and looked around. The smoke quickly grew thick, choking her, and the heat intense. She staggered to the door and tried to push it open but it would not open. She pounded with her fists even as the smoke poured in under the door and clouded the room, burning her throat and stinging her eyes, choking as if she were drowning in the heat and smoke.

"Help, help!" she cried with her last ounce of strength and will. The propped chair on the other side of the door held it fast even as it, too, was being consumed by the hot licking flames that had spread quickly licking at the coal oil that had been splashed on walls and flooring.

Her blows to free herself became weaker. Her cries became like those of a mewing kitten. And then there were no more sounds from inside the room that was simply a deathtrap.

Outside in the yard, Bo Wilson watched his handiwork, watched as the flames licked through the windows of shattering smoked glass, as smoke curled up around the eaves in gray, swollen tongues, the bright licking flames of fire chasing after.

He'd heard her first screams inside, the tin box of money held in his hand like a prize he'd won at a fair. His father's money. His money now. And at last the screams stopped and there was only the sound of crashing timber as the house began to collapse inward on itself in bright orange, glorious flames.

He neither saw nor heard the rider so transfixed was he on the fire scene. Not until someone shouted: "What the hell's going on?"

He turned to see a man close to his own age running toward him, a loose-reined horse standing behind him. The man had a pistol drawn in his hand, aiming it.

Bo dropped the box in reaching for his own gun, the heated air creating a wind that scattered the loose money like spooked birds.

"I just seen the fire!" he yelped. "Somebody's in there!"

The ruse didn't work on the other man. He shot Bo Wilson once through the forehead before the Wilson boy could clear his piece. Tom had shot without a second thought, then he ran past the dead man to the house. But the heat kept him at bay. Still he did his best to enter and burned his hands in the doing and was chased back out into the yard.

He called her name—"Woman! Woman!"— but there was only the sound of crackling wood. "God damn!" he swore.

Tom Moon squatted in the dust and cursed, his hands badly blistered, but he did not feel the pain as he watched the flames finish eating away the last of his father's house and what he could not even imagine inside. He cursed and cursed.

He should have forced her to go with him to Red Pony the other day when he'd come out, he told himself. He should have stayed with her until his father returned. He blamed himself not for her murder, but for not being forceful enough to have prevented it. He told himself that Cole would not have made the same mistake.

The paper birds of money fluttered to the ground around him with the dying heat. *It is all just a waste,* he thought, *money and the things men will do for it. Just a damned stupid waste!*

CHAPTER EIGHTEEN

John Henry Cole saw her coming out of Karl's Liberty Palace Saloon. No one could miss a woman like that, he thought. Even if Wilson hadn't showed him her photograph, Cole believed he would have recognized her. She was different from all the others, more stately and regal in appearance, tall and willowy with a bearing uncommon to the wives of other men. Cole could see why Wilson wanted her back so badly. He watched as she crossed the street and entered a millinery shop with ladies hats in the window: hats decorated with the latest in bird feathers, egrets and pheasant.

He waited to see if Lucky Jack or The Gimp came out of Karl's Liberty Palace Saloon to follow her. Neither did.

He walked over and waited outside the millinery shop, rolled a shuck, and smoked it. When she came out, carrying a stringed box, he said: "Pardon me, Missus Wilson."

She stopped short and looked at him, startled.

"Excuse me?" she said.

"You are Missus Wilson," he said.

She looked uncertain, glanced across the way at Karl's Liberty Palace Saloon's front doors then upward toward the extended porch on the second floor. Its chair was empty.

"Who are you?" she said.

He told her and why he was there, then added: "I'd like a private word with you."

"There must be some mistake," she said.

"No mistake. Your husband showed me a photograph of the two of you."

She purposely acted confused, uncertain, but said nothing.

"An observation," he said. "Looks to me like you're no more a hostage than I am."

She looked as if she wanted to run.

"You say the word and I'll go back and tell Wilson he was wrong about you," Cole affirmed.

"It's not so simple as you seem to think, Mister Cole."

"Then why don't you tell me how it is?"

"You don't understand that I'm under threat of death if I say or do the wrong thing," she said.

"Like shop for hats, you mean, when you're supposed to be kidnapped by one of the worst men in the West. Is that what you mean?"

"I can't be seen talking with you," she insisted.

"And if you are?"

"He will kill us both."

"No, ma'am, he won't."

"How can *you* be so certain?"

"This," he said, lifting the coach gun slightly. 'And this, too." He pulled back the flap of his

231

coat to show her the hanging iron riding in his shoulder rig.

"You're only one man."

"I'm all I need to be, Missus Wilson. This wouldn't be my first dance."

"You seem awfully sure of yourself."

"I know my abilities. Now do you want to tell me what's going on here?"

"It's true. I was kidnapped off the train by Lucky and his bunch. And I want to be released unharmed. My husband sent a Pinkerton to bring me back, but Lucky or one of his men killed him. So Lucky sent another demand to my husband, had me write it out, and he's been waiting for him to come with the money. I guess that's you."

"I have to say something, ma'am. Your story sounds like a bunch of horse shit, but for the parts that could be true."

She acted shocked but he knew she wasn't.

"May we step around into the alley where we're not so conspicuous? He can see me from up there," she said. "And Lucky's got spies all over town."

"Sure."

He followed her into the nearest alley, and down it.

"OK, I'm still listening," Cole said once they paused.

She took a moment, then said: "Lucky and I go back a ways. This was all his idea, to get a rich

232

nan's money. Any rich man, it didn't matter. It was my duty to snag one, get him to marry me. Wilson was that man. At first I was OK with t, but then after a time of being with Wilson, I came to like him. He treated me like a real lady and someone special. I tried to get Lucky to call t off, but he wouldn't listen. To tell you the truth, Mister Cole, I'm afraid of Lucky, his potential for violence and what he'd do to me if I refused him. So I went along with it. . . ."

He tried to discern the veracity in her story. Some of it seemed to make sense. "Go on," he said.

Some riders trotted past the head of the alley and she looked out toward them with a fearful gaze.

"Lucky aims to send me back all right, but then he's going to kill Mister Wilson and his boys and leave me the grieving widow, but one who inherits everything."

"Then he swoops in and the two of you marry and live happy ever after, that it?"

"Yes, but I don't trust Lucky any longer. He'll do to me what he'd do to Wilson, and then he would inherit everything as the grieving widower." Her face was etched with real fear now. "So, if you've come to take me back, I'm ready to go with you, Mister Cole."

"What about Wilson?" he said. "You aiming to tell him the truth of your scheme?"

She nodded, her eyes brimming with tears. " am. I'll take my chances that he'll forgive me i I'm truthful."

"Something you should know," Cole said "He's dying."

She looked up, knuckling a tear from the corner of one eye. Fake or not, Cole couldn't tell.

"I kinda figured he might be," she said. "He complained of pain sometimes."

"His boy, Bo, told me you and he had a liaison more than once . . . that true?"

She nodded. "I admit that I am a woman who needs physical love. And when Mister Wilson could not give it to me, he gave me permission to find it elsewhere as long as I was discreet about it. I know it was wrong, but I figured that by being with Bo it would be kept private, that the son would not hurt his father by telling him. I know it was a terrible betrayal, but even that I'm willing to confess."

"You seem to have made a lot of mistakes."

"Have you ever made any mistakes?"

"Yeah, a bunch, but not all at one time."

"All I ask is that you let Mister Wilson and God be my judge, Mister Cole."

"Fair enough," he agreed. "You willing to go back with me on the flyer when it comes through tonight?"

"Yes," she said.

"Then be at the station."

"I will."

She held out a hand for him to shake but he simply said: "I'll see you at the station tonight."

He watched her go, then went on one last errand he'd set for himself, to find a man named Gardiner, the one who'd killed Nell Blue. It hadn't taken much asking around to locate the fellow. He was the local and only preacher and his church stood at the farthest point at the west end of town, a simple white clapboard building without so much as a steeple or a bell to ring in the sheaves. Next to it was a small house of similar construction but with a picket fence and flower boxes but no flowers that time of year.

He knocked on the door and a horse-faced woman answered.

Cole asked for Mister Gardiner.

"I'm his wife," she said. "He is next door at the church, preparing for next Wednesday's sermon."

"Thank you, ma'am."

He went, now far from certain what exactly he would do when he found the man, but knowing that he aimed to do something.

He entered the church's double front doors and stood in a room empty but for several benches without backs, here and there, upon their seats worn hymnals collecting dust, awaiting voices. There was no one there, or so he thought at first. But then a sound in the back came from an off room, a sound like someone in pain. He went to the off room with its closed door, the outer light falling through a double row of windows on either side of the church's walls, falling upon the empty benches with their hymnals.

There were voices within the room. Pained voices.

Cole turned the doorknob and flicked the door open.

Upon a small table lay a woman, her skirts up, her legs spread, and between them a man stood, his black trousers gathered at his feet. The woman was the one who made the sounds, but not sounds of pain, rather of pleasure, her eyes clamped shut, her mouth not so much. The man turned his head at the unexpected intrusion.

"You must be Gardiner," Cole said.

The man was uncertain as to what to do about a stranger holding a shotgun in one hand. "Oh, God!" he said.

"Not exactly," Cole said, and cracked him hard across the face with the gun's stock.

"That's for Nell Blue," Cole said. He looked at the woman who was quickly gathering herself. She was no better-looking than a mud hen. "I guess you were hoping for the short road to heaven," he said.

CHAPTER NINETEEN

The mule was gone. Rita May had emerged first from the wagon the night after leaving John Henry Cole in Gun Town. She and Kate had traveled a few miles outside of the town's limits, then wearily set up camp, and a cold camp it was, too. Neither of the women felt much like speaking to the other. Having found Cole had changed things between them and threatened to wreck their plans of a life together without men. Both of them had been attracted to Cole, each in her own way and for different reasons and needs, and both of them knew it about the other, but had left it completely unsaid so that the tension was thick. Although Rita May had made a subtle attempt to patch things up with Kate that evening in the wagon, Kate wasn't in any mood to do any patching. She blamed Rita May for having gotten rid of Cole too soon.

"Don't!" she'd said when Rita May reached for her in the darkness.

Rita May withdrew her hand as if she'd been burned, and lay there in silence. She wondered about men in her history of them, dating back to her first one, a brother who, when they were kids, had assaulted her in a barn haymow. It was Edward, or Little Eddy as everyone called him, who had broken her like a dropped vase by forcing himself on her. His hurt to her had been more than physical and it had branded her in her mind as not deserving of anything better than a certain amount of cruelty from men. Eddy had called her a "big ol' tomboy." And certainly it seemed from that point on that the only men she found attractive were the cruel and profane ones. She seemed to grow into a certain mannishness, as if it were the only way to fight on even ground those who would take advantage of her. She only understood one thing about men—they'd do it with anything alive, if given the chance, and perhaps a few even with anything that was once alive. It was later, as a young woman, that she discovered the pleasures of other women, at least one other woman, a neighbor's wife. It wasn't so much the physical part—she could do without any of that—as it was the kindliness and gentleness that she'd been shown, the understanding of all her anxiety about men and the world in which men lived that had seduced her. The other woman's name was Martha and she was as plain as a plastered wall in looks, a large woman with a bundle of premature iron-gray hair, but kindly eyes. She was soft-spoken, a woman who seemed to carry the burdens of life on her shoulders but with great strength and understanding. Martha had had a brood of wild young ones that were in constant ruckus, always fighting and chasing one another and raising seven kinds of hell. But Martha had a way with them that could gentle them right down when she needed to do so. Martha had a husband twenty years her senior, a former riverboat captain who'd given up the ever changing waterways to search for silver, who was forever away in the search of the elusive gleaming veins through hard rock, and would only come home now and again just long enough to produce another child with her, then go off again. He always found just enough silver to keep on looking, to keep on going, to keep a household together by sending her a little money. Thank God for the chickens and cow and large garden.

Rita May and Martha's intertwining came about so naturally it did not seem at all *unnatural*. As neighbors they were in constant consultation and communion, discussing this and that and understanding the burdens of a woman, and wives in general, baking breads and fixing meals. The first kiss was natural, too, and so was everything that followed. Before she knew it, Rita May had fallen in love with Martha, a love she'd never before experienced, a gentle sort of love that demanded nothing of her, that was like the wind when it touched her hair or the softness of rain when it fell at night.

But then Martha's silver-seeking husband heard of a large silver strike in Nevada and moved them all away, kit and caboodle, and with them went Rita May's heart. Until she met Kate who, along with her husband, Slim, moved into the vacated house. And so it had come to pass, but this time Rita May had to admit that her love of Kate felt forced, felt more as a need to fill the void Martha's absence had left than something natural, and the wind no longer touched her hair and the rain no longer fell at night for her in the way it had with Martha. And when they had found John Henry Cole, Rita May was fearful that he would fracture the tenuous bond between her and Kate that Rita May had hoped to build into something stronger, something more truthful. There was something she sensed rather than saw in Cole that reminded her of the kindness of Martha. Maybe that was it. That *had* to be it.

Kate, on the other hand, had never been sure of her alliance with Rita May. For her, Rita May was a refuge from Slim, from a life of dull routine and looking into the mirror, of growing into a grim-faced woman aged before her time, faded as an old gingham dress scrubbed too often and hung too long in the sun. Dead at forty. For Kate, Rita May represented adventure, a new world. But Cole had changed all that for her, too, and she couldn't even say why except that Cole represented a new world to her, the same sort of adventure that Rita May had, only in a more natural way. Such were the workings of heart and soul that cast the two of them into the uneasy silence.

"Kate!" Rita May called in the morning. "Come out here!"

Kate clambered out of the wagon, looking disheveled, her eyes red from lack of sleep and crying—crying that Rita May had listened to half the night, a crying that was like hot drops of lead against her own heart, for Rita May knew she had somehow hurt the vulnerable Kate badly.

"What is it?" Kate said, her arms folded across her chest, defiant at anything Rita May had to say.

"The mule's been stolen."

"Didn't you hobble it?"

"Of course I did. Look, the hobbles lay there in the grass, you ninny!"

"What is there to do?" Kate said.

"No choice I can see but walk back to that town?"

Kate said nothing for a moment, thinking. "Yes," she said then. "It's the best thing to do."

"Good, then we'll take what few things we can carry and possibly find someone in that town who would be willing to buy a wagon full of the professor's elixirs."

"And then what?" Kate wanted to know.

Rita May shrugged. "I suppose we'll figure it out at the time."

They gathered their valises, and Rita May

wanting to take some samples, put in a few bottles of the cure-all. They started back toward Gun Town.

Later, when John Henry Cole saw them coming up the boardwalk together, he felt a surge of something, seeing them again. He approached them.

"What are you two doing here?" he asked.

"Someone stole the mule," Rita May said.

"I'm exhausted," Kate said. "My feet hurt and I'm dying of thirst."

Cole led them to the German café and sat them at a table. The cook, Peck, came with a bit of a surprised look on his face, gazing at the trio, and said to Cole: "By golly, it didn't take you long to find companionship."

Rita May cast him an angry glance and said: "Please bring us something cold to drink and something warm to eat. You do understand what I'm saying, don't you?"

He flinched at her sharpness. "Yes ma'am." He went.

"Can you help us, Mister Cole?" Kate said, dabbing her damp cheeks with a small white hanky with tatted fringe.

"You mean to get your mule back?"

"No, with selling the wagon and its contents so that we might have money to travel on."

"I can try."

Rita May remained silent, not looking at Cole.

When Peck returned with glasses of tea and bowls of beef stew, Kate asked: "Do you have facilities here?"

"Out back is where, ma'am."

"Thank you," she said, and excused herself from the table and followed Peck to the back door he held open for her, thinking she was a mighty pert woman.

"So," Cole said, "you're going to sell the wagon, which I'm guessing you don't actually own since you don't look like a professor named Pickle."

"That's right."

"You mind my asking how you came by it in the first place?"

"You can ask whatever you like, but I can choose not to answer."

"Another mystery," he said.

"Pardon me?"

"I meant to say that you are indeed a mysterious woman."

"And that troubles you in some manner?"

"No. It only makes me curious."

"About what?"

She sipped from the glass of tea. The cook had chipped ice off a block with an ice pick and put it in the tea to cool it, and the coldness had the refreshing capacity to join body and soul again after a long hot walk.

"About you," he said.

She leveled her gaze at Cole over the rim of the glass. "Is it curiosity or attraction?"

"Could be a bit of both."

"You mean to say you don't have a wife waiting back home for you?"

"Yes, ma'am, I do, well, sort of . . . not officially."

"Typical man, I'd say you are, Mister Cole, always looking for the greener grass."

He felt a bit guilty. He always considered himself a faithful man, but a man nonetheless who was prone to mistakes of the heart and mind. Still, he could not deny his curiosity or his attraction toward this seemingly unknowable woman.

"Maybe so," he said. "But I'd like to think otherwise about myself."

Kate returned.

There was a silence as they ate.

"I'll see what I can do about getting your wagon sold," Cole said finally. "But I'm leaving on the midnight flyer, so if I can't find you a buyer, you will be on your own."

Both women looked glumly disappointed.

He stood away from the table.

"How is your head?" Kate asked, hoping to delay the parting for a bit.

"It's good," he said. "Thanks for asking. I'll let you know about a buyer if I find one."

Peck couldn't help but overhear the conversation. He said: "I know of someone who might be willing to buy the ladies' wagon. Harkness over at the livery. Always buying and selling transportation."

"Thanks," Cole said. "I'll check it out."

They watched him go. An elderly couple came in, and Peck went off to serve them.

"Let's just hope the liveryman is interested in buying the wagon," Rita May said.

"How *did* you ever come by that wagon to begin with?" Kate asked. "You never did say the first time I asked you."

"Let's just say I got a man drunk on his own cure-all and made him promises I did not keep."

"So we're wanted women for more than just fleeing our husbands?"

"More than wanted," Rita May said with a sardonic smile.

Kate shook her head.

"I should have told you sooner," Rita May said.

"We ought to just go into bank robbing, I mean if we're going to be wanted women." Kate offered a surprised smile.

"You mean wanton wanted women?" Rita May replied, the ice between them broken.

"Yes, precisely."

"How can we get guns?"

"The same way you got that wagon I suppose," Kate said.

"Well, now you sound like a woman after my own heart."

"Rooting, tooting, gun-shooting wild women."

They both laughed.

Peck had finished his service to the elderly couple and now stood looking on at the two women from his cubby, a cigarette dangling from his mouth, the ashes falling into the stew to add flavor.

Now there are a couple of exciting women, he thought. *Not like the local belles with their slatternly looks and ways*. His imagination flowed like hot gravy over mashed spuds. *I don't suppose either is looking for a husband, but maybe I should ask just the same.*

It had been a very long time since Peck had found himself wrapped in the loving arms of a loving woman. A very long time.

CHAPTER TWENTY

A man arrived on a black stud horse and brought a telegram to the porch and handed it to the housekeeper. "This here is for Mister Wilson, Miz Foster."

She thanked him and carried the letter to Wilson where he lay abed on a mattress stuffed with goose down in a well-lit room because of all the floor to ceiling windows.

"Carter brought this," she said, handing him the still folded telegram. "He said it was for you."

"Read it to me, please," Wilson said.

But for the prescribed dosage of laudanum Wilson did not think he could stand the pain that seemed ever increasing in his lower bowels. He regretted having to die. The world was such a wondrous place, with such days as this one, with a soft warm wind blowing into his room and the sun bright and clean and clear, that he hated the thought of never experiencing it again.

But worse, he missed Lenora terribly, and the thought that such a young and vibrant woman had had to suffer at the hands of murderers left him nearly breathless. He tried hard not to imagine what she'd gone through, how she must have suffered before they killed her. And for what? Money? Hell, he would have given everything he had to have gotten her back.

He waited for Mrs. Foster to read the telegram. She read it in silence to herself, her lips moving, then she lowered it in one hand and said simply: "Bo has been killed."

He closed his eyes. He said: "When and where?"

"This is from the marshal in Red Pony," she said. "Marshal Tom Moon."

He swallowed hard. He always suspected that someday the boy would come to a bad end, but not so soon in life, not before him. "Did the marshal give details?"

"I don't think it matters, Mister Wilson. It really shouldn't. It will only cause you to fret and take its further toll on your health. Why not let me get you a cup of tea?"

"No! Damn it! I want to know what happened to my son."

"He burned down a house with a woman in it," she said softly, "and the marshal shot and killed him in the act. He wants to know if you want Bo's body shipped home or to have him buried there?" Her hands were trembling by the time she finished.

Wilson took the news coldly. He already knew who the woman in the burned house was, the wife of John Henry Cole—the man he had hired to find Lenora and who had left the money with his woman.

"Why?" he said softly.

"Why what, sir?"

He opened his eyes and looked at her, the saddest eyes she'd ever looked into, so sad it forced her to cross herself.

"He would have had everything, why did he need a few lousy dollars more? Why would he risk his life for the money? It makes no bloody sense!"

"I'll go and get you some tea," she said, wishing to retreat from the room.

He lifted a hand to stop her. "Please tell Jesse to come up, and leave the telegram," he said in a wavering voice.

"Yes, sir."

Presently the younger son was watching one of the cowhands trying to break an ornery stud horse. The horse had scraped the cowhand off twice and bucked him off once, but the cowhand, with the help of another waddy, had snubbed the stud up tight to the snubbing post and put a blindfold over its eyes before getting on him again, then told his pard to cut him loose. This time the cowhand stuck until he had the stud into a trot around the corral, breaking it to the bit and rein, gentling it down without breaking its spirit. Jesse stood in awe of these men, these horse-breakers. He hadn't the nerve to climb aboard one of the rough stock.

Mrs. Foster came from the house and said: "Your father wants to see you."

"Yes, ma'am," he said.

He walked back to the house with her, but he climbed the stairs alone, and entered his dying father's room.

"Pa?"

Wilson looked at the boy who was less a spitting image of him than Bo, who looked more like his mother, darker, more blunted features. "I need you to catch the train to Red Pony," the old man said, his voice cracking with phlegm and subdued sadness. "Your brother has been killed and I want you to escort his body home."

Jesse said nothing at first. It seemed impossible to him that his brother was dead. Bo had always been the stronger one of the two, the bolder and more dangerous. It just couldn't be he was dead. "How?"

Wilson nodded toward the telegram and handed it to Jesse who read it with dismay.

"You know," Wilson began, "he went off on his own after we got back here, saying as how he was going to Bozeman to look for more blooded stock. Well, he went to that house of the man we hired . . . Cole . . . and apparently set the place on fire with his woman in it. For the money is the only reason I can imagine."

Jesse wasn't so sure it hadn't been from pure meanness, but this time he remained silent.

Wilson had spoken, looking out the window at a thing he could not see, at the sunlight bright and bold and painful to look at—the sun that splayed itself over hay fields like golden water. The curtains lifted and fell and he recalled better days in this room—first with his late wife, and later with his second wife, the younger one, the one he thought would always bring him happiness until this very moment when he was dying. "You will go?" he asked.

"Yes, Pa, I'll go."

"Go first to the telegraph office and wire that marshal that you're coming and to preserve the body of your dead brother, and then catch the train."

"Yes, Pa."

"Bring him home where he belongs. In spite of whatever he did or might have done, he is still my son, as you are my son, and now my *only* son. It's all up to you now, Jesse. . . ."

Then as a wind-up toy whose spring had unwound, Wilson fell silent, and closed his eyes, and for a moment Jesse wondered if his father had not died, but then he saw the slight rise and fall of his chest, almost in concert with the wind-blown curtains.

"I'll go now," he said.

CHAPTER TWENTY-ONE

"I seen that bitch talking to your pal, John Henry, out front of the ladies' hat shop," Gypsy said.

Lucky was drinking in the saloon and consorting with a young, rather chubby gal calling herself Little Eva, a platinum-haired whore newly arrived in Gun Town and looking for fast employment. As usual, Lucky was interested in any new flesh that hit town and saw it as his duty and responsibility to make sure she was up to the job. Thus far he had only been chatting with her. He knew he had to be clever so that Miss High and Mighty didn't learn of his philandering and raise holy hell. He'd just about had it with her anyway, but he needed to keep her in harness until the full plan was carried out.

"That so?" Lucky said.

"Chatting like a couple of magpies on a telegraph wire."

"What do you think they were talking about?"

"What do *you* think they were talking about is the better question."

"Go ask her," Lucky said.

"She upstairs?"

"Seen her come in a while ago."

The Gimp started for the stairs.

Lucky warned him: "No rough stuff with her, you understand?"

"I understand," Gypsy said. "Perfectly."

He entered the room without knocking.

Lenora stood facing him with a small pepper-box pistol in her hand.

"I heard you coming down the hallway, that walk of yours," she said, "and this time I'm ready for you."

He held up his hands, palms outward. "Whoa!"

"You can just turn around and leave, or get a face full of lead."

"Lucky asked me to come and ask you what you were talking to Cole about."

"I wasn't."

"Like hell, I seen you."

"You're as much a weasel as you look."

"You thinking about leaving Lucky? Because if you are, I might have a plan of my own."

"You think I care to hear it?"

"You might."

"I doubt it."

"You can't tell me you didn't like it . . . the other day."

He offered a wicked grin and she pulled the trigger, the bullet hitting him in the left palm of the proffered hand. He yelped like a scalded dog nearly causing her to laugh aloud.

"That tell you if I liked it or not? Get out of my room!"

He cursed her, calling her every name an angry man could call a woman.

She said: "Just keep it up and I'll shoot you again."

"No, no, damn it!" Blood dripped from his shot hand like red rain and fell *plit-plat* onto the carpet.

Lucky heard the gunshot and took to the stairs, the new whore following right behind him. He rushed in while Little Eva stopped and stood in the open doorway.

"What the hell did you shoot him for?" he asked Lenora, as Gypsy did a little gimpy jig as he held one hand with the other.

"He called me vile names," she said.

"Not true, god damn it!" Gypsy said in a high-pitched voice.

"He's a piece of trash," Lenora said, "and I want him hauled out of my room."

Lucky Jack looked from one to the other. Lenora was staring at the new girl who stood stockstill in the doorway as if fascinated by the goings on, the sight of blood.

"Go on and get, too," Lenora said to Lucky, "and take your new whore with you."

"I want to know what you were talking to Cole about," Lucky said angrily.

"Get me a damn' doctor before I bleed to death," Gypsy pleaded.

"What do you think I was talking to him about," she said.

"You're not leaving, not without my permission. You know the plan, Lenora. And we're sticking to the plan."

"I know you're a lying, cheating, no good son-of-a-bitch," she said, "and I've got my own plan, and it's not to stick around here with you. Maybe *she* can take my place in your schemes from now on!" Lenora jutted her chin toward the woman with the gleaming whitish hair, the bunched bosoms threatening to loose themselves from the bodice of her low-cut dress. She was younger and just as pretty as Lenora.

"By the time I get done, there won't be nobody for you to leave with, and I'm about sick of you anyhow. I'm going to finish that old man and his boys and me and you are going to get wedded up, then what's yours is mine. Now stay put!"

She pulled the trigger again, hoping this time to put a slug into Lucky but it misfired and he crossed the room quickly as a cat and jerked the pepperbox from her hand and slapped her hard across the face.

"No more!" he said. Turning toward the other one he said: "Eva, you stay here and keep an eye on her and don't let her leave." Then he worked the mechanism on the pepperbox, turning the cylinder till the hammer was set on a live round and handed it to the new girl.

"She tries anything, shoot her in the legs, both of 'em. Come on, Gypsy."

"I'm bleeding like a stuck hog!"

"We'll get Doc to patch you up."

Gypsy tossed Lenora one last vile look before they left.

Lenora glared at the new whore. "You won't shoot me," she said.

With confidence the new girl said: "The hell I won't."

CHAPTER TWENTY-TWO

John Henry Cole had gone to the livery stable and was negotiating the sale of the medicine wagon with the liveryman, Harkness.

"Medicine wagon, you say?" the owner replied as he scratched in a tangle of beard that ended at the middle button of his waistcoat.

"Yes, and several boxes of elixir thrown in."

"What's it good for, the elixir, I mean?"

"Just about everything, whatever ails you."

"*Humph* . . . doubt that."

"The women who have it had their mule stolen," Cole explained. "They need the money to advance their journey. Two young women going to San Francisco to join a nunnery and do God's work."

A lie of course, but sometimes a little lie was necessary. How many times had he told a lie in the old days to catch a miscreant? Some deputies working for Judge Parker even took to wearing disguises. Old Shurm Lewis wore a lady's dress and Mother Hubbard bonnet in order to round up Wallace Bigfoot and his gang.

The man scratched more in his beard. It could have hidden several crows.

"What they asking for it?"

Cole shrugged. "Make an offer?"

"Hard to say without seeing it," he said.

Cole told him where he could go and look at it.

"All right, I'll ride out there later on with Enid, my boy, and we'll look it over and I'll let you know."

"You can find the women at the café."

Cole went in search of Rita May and Kate but was intercepted by Lucky Jack and The Gimp who now had a bandaged hand.

"I thought I made it clear," Lucky said, "that she's not leaving without I get paid for her."

"Yeah, he made it clear," Gypsy echoed.

"You made it clear," Cole said.

"Then what the hell is the problem? Why are you not minding your own damned business?"

Cole raised the coach gun he carried in his right hand. "You want to make a fight of it, Lucky, me with this street-sweeper?"

"You in or you out, that's what I want to know, Cole?"

"I am whatever I choose to be and it's none of your damned affair."

"Then we'll have a fight."

"Nothing like the present," Cole said, leveling the barrels at both men. "Make your play."

He saw The Gimp take an awkward step backward, but Lucky Jack was a cooler customer and showed no fear of being halved by the shotgun.

"Not here, not now, but at my choosing. You'll be dead before the flyer comes in and the only way you'll leave on it is in a box. You might think that coach gun and that pistol you carry is enough, but they ain't nearly enough for what I'll throw at you."

"You do what you have to do, Lucky, but right now you're in my way."

The Gimp looked nervous but Lucky Jack had the impassive countenance of a man waiting to go to an ice cream social.

"You made a long trip for nothing more than your own funeral."

"Maybe so, but you'll be joining me in the grave . . . him, too."

"It could have been so easy," Lucky said. "You could have thrown in with me and you'd never know such a sweet life. Whatever Wilson's paying you, it ain't enough."

"Maybe not, Lucky, but you know me, I don't quit a job when I hire on."

"Yeah, I know you, Cole."

"Clear the decks."

Lucky and Gypsy stepped aside, and when Cole passed them and was several feet away, Gypsy went to pull his pistol but Lucky stayed his hand.

"You do and he'll unload that double load of buckshot into us both."

"You getting soft on me, Lucky?"

"Just trying to keep you from getting the rest of your parts blown off."

"Shit."

"Let's go get the others."

"Not before I ask you when the hell was it you asked him to join up with us."

"At the café."

"You never said nothing to me about it."

Lucky Jack leveled a hard stare at the smaller man. "Since when do I need to consult you about anything?"

"Just saying. I've been covering your back for a long time."

"You want to move on, be my guest."

"Ah, Lucky . . . don't be like that now."

Lucky Jack started up the street, and The Gimp wondered if now might not be the time to kill him, but there was the slightest bit of doubt in his feral heart because he'd seen Lucky in gun action before and knew the man to have almost a sixth sense. No, best to wait for a better time, a sure enough time. So he limped along hurriedly and caught up to his master, like a three-legged dog, trotting.

Cole found the women still sitting in the café, the cook-waiter, Peck, entertaining them with stories about his days as an Indian fighter with Custer's 7th Calvary.

"Tell us more," Kate was saying when Cole entered.

"I might have found you a buyer for your wagon," Cole announced, taking up an empty chair. "I could stand a cup of coffee," he said to Peck. Peck went quickly to get a pot and returned with it and some cups.

Two men entered the café, spurs ringing, hats knocked back off their foreheads. They looked like cowpunchers in their vests and dungarees, leather cuffs, and quirts. They each had a revolver set butt forward in a holster and their clothes were dusty and boots run down at the heels. They took seats and called for coffee. Peck went, got them some, then came and sat down with Cole and the women.

Cole explained about the liveryman after pouring himself some of the Arbuckle's. "If that liveryman asks, you two are on your way to San Francisco to join a nunnery."

Rita May arched a brow as she looked at him.

"Oh," Peck said to Kate mostly. "Pardon me, na'am, I didn't realize you two was such devoted Christians."

"We're not," Rita May said. "Hardly."

Peck looked relieved.

Kate laughed. "Oh, that we were."

"I've got trouble on my hands and I need you two to steer clear of me for as long as you're in town." Cole also told them where the livery was and to follow up on their own.

"Why?" Rita May said. "What's going on?"

"It's Lucky and them, ain't it?" Peck blurted.

"Yeah," Cole said, reaching for his makings.

"I don't understand," Rita May said. "Who's Lucky . . . and *them?*"

"Nothing I can't handle. I just don't want the two of you to get caught in the middle."

Peck stared at the coach gun Cole had laid across the table.

"You want, I can handle that for you," Peck said.

Cole looked at him. He hadn't heard the story of the cook's survival with Reno on the Little Bighorn about which he'd told the women earlier. "No, sir, best you keep to doing what you're doing. You got a nice little life here."

"I killed men before," Peck quickly said.

"He has, Mister Cole. Mister Peck was just telling us about . . . ," Kate put in.

"Leave it be," Rita May interrupted. "Let's stay out of any more trouble than what we've already got."

Kate offered her an offended and hurtful look.

"There's not many, if any, who'll back you in this town," Peck said.

"I know it," Cole said, twisting off the ends of his newly made cigarette.

Kate looked from one man to the other.

Cole struck a match and lit his cigarette. Eyeing the two cowpunchers who'd come in, he noticed they were casting sidelong glances. Maybe it was the women they were checking out, maybe not. At this point, he trusted no one. "Soon as you can," he said. "Clear out of this town."

He stood away from the table, took up the coach gun, and cradled it in the crook of his arm. He did it to show the two cowpunchers and anyone else that he was armed and dangerous. "You all take care," he said.

Cole had no sooner left than the cowpunchers got up and left. Peck took notice and said: "I wonder if I might impose on you for a favor."

"Sure," Kate said. "What?"

Rita May was already shaking her head no.

"Could you keep an eye on this place for a bit. I think maybe your friend is in trouble and could use me out there."

"Yes, of course," Kate said before Rita May could voice her objection.

"I'll be back as soon as I can, and if I ain't, there'll be a job opening here for either one of you if you can cook."

With that Peck headed for the kitchen, untying his apron as he went and tossing it across a chair. He disappeared out the back.

Cole went up the first alley he came to after leaving the café. He went to the end and turned down a back alley that ran along the rear of the establishments. The sun was directly overhead and the alley stank of garbage, and when the wind shifted in a certain direction the air was even more rife with the stench. Several cur dogs were sniffing around the garbage cans and paused to look at the two-legged intruder. Cole knew he was officially a hunted man now, that Lucky Jack probably had half the town's guns looking for him. If he could hold out until the flyer came in and get on it, he might stand a chance. His concern, too, was if Lenora Wilson could make it. Otherwise, there would be blood and plenty of it.

He wanted to find Bill Hammer, in fading hopes that the old lawman might be able to raise a few honest men to back his play. It wasn't much of a hope, but it was all Cole had.

CHAPTER TWENTY-THREE

Peck entered the gunsmith's in a rush. "Abe, I need a shotgun 'cause I can't hit shit with any other kind of firearm with just one eyeball in my head . . . throws off my depth perception."

"Pecker, why you need to hit anything in the first place?"

" 'Cause there is going to be a killing or maybe quite a lot of killing here before the day is out, and I aim to be in on it."

"That so? And what'd you do to bring down such troubles on your head?"

The two were old friends and often played checkers late at night over a wood barrel there in the store and drank sipping whiskey while regaling each other with tales of former lives. Both men had been veterans of the great conflict, Peck for the South and Abe for the Northern cause. The gunsmith had seen plenty of bloody action at places like Kolb's Farm, Malvern Hill, and Gettysburg. He had been a sniper, could kill at long range and short, and had. His love of guns had not abated after the war but he had little blood frenzy in him since those days.

"They're gonna kill a fellow today, Lucky Jack and them."

"I think I know the fellow you mean . . . was in here earlier. Bought a coach gun off me. Tall fellow, that the one?"

"That's him."

"What they gonna kill him for?"

"A woman."

"They wouldn't be the first to kill over a woman."

"This one Lucky stole and this fellow, this Cole aims to get her back to her husband."

"Well, if Lucky's got her, then it sure enough will be a killing day. What sort of shotgun you want, gauge-wise, I mean? I got Twelves and Tens, even got a goose gun. Would a goose gun do you?"

"Too damn' heavy. Give me a twelve-gauge and plenty of shells for it."

The gunsmith reached behind him and took down a heavy Whitney double-barrel and hefted it to Peck, then grabbed a box of shells from the counter and set those down, too.

"How you aim on paying for 'em?" the gunsmith said.

"In blood," Peck said.

"No doubt. But I'm not the United States government handing out guns for my health."

"Oh, hell, you'll get it back, if slightly grimed up. Let's just say I'll rent it from you."

"Well, I'm coming along just to make sure my property don't get absconded with," the gunsmith said, removing his oily leather apron and coming around the corner of the gun case.

"You best bring a gun then."

The gunsmith shook his head. "I take a gun, I'm liable to be forced to use it."

"You don't take a gun and you might wish you had."

"Well, maybe you're right . . . just for self-protection," the gunsmith said, grabbing a sporting rifle with tang sights.

Out they went.

Lucky told Gypsy to get Lee Reynolds and Hasty Parker and Tom Mulligan and anyone else he could find who was in town and not dead drunk. "Bring them over to the Liberty."

Gypsy didn't care much for taking orders any more from Lucky, but he'd do it, he told himself, in hopes there was to be one hellacious shoot-out and maybe Lucky would either get killed or badly wounded to the point where he could finish him off right proper.

"Already sent Billy Pepper and Rockwell to dog him," Gypsy said.

"That's good," Lucky said. "Maybe they'll have him down and out by the time we catch up."

Gypsy went in search of the other three, figuring two of them would be laid up with whores and the other one—Tom Mulligan—would be lying drunk in his tent.

· · ·

John Henry Cole found Bill Hammer sitting alone in his small cramped office full of heat and dust, tugging on a bottle of Old Tub, and muttering to himself, lost in the reverie of headier times when youth sprang eternal and Bill was yet a handsome soldier of the law. It was his habit on most days to try and recall the names of the lovers he'd had as a young man, to scribble them down on a piece of paper, the back of a Wanted dodger, an old envelope, or just any piece of paper he could find. Each time he made an attempt to calculate an accurate figure, and even though he'd forgotten most of their names, there were still those whose memory stood out as if he'd just met them yesterday. He always set about to recount them in the order in which he had met them and under what circumstances—the pert Nancy in Omaha, Callie in Hays, and Jenny in Waycross, Georgia that time. His heart heaved and sighed like a frigate in rough seas as he recalled them, and it had turned into a sea of regret and loss and no longer one of adventure.

He sat on a harp-back wood chair, unpainted but worn smooth from so many having sat on it, garters on his shirt sleeves, and his striped trousers tucked down into his mule-ear boots when he was shaken from his reverie as Cole entered, the stub of a pencil pressed between thumb and forefinger.

"They're gunning for you, ain't they?" Bill said.

Cole nodded, glancing out the lone window of the tiny office. "Can I count on you, Bill?"

Bill set down the pencil on the paper with partial names of women who, for whatever reason, had shared with him their warm and lovely bodies and were now simply a black scribble in crumbling lead, as lost to the world as he was. A not uncommon thought always lingered in his mind as he wrote the names. *Do they ever think of me?*

"No, I don't reckon you can, John Henry. I wish I could state otherwise, but that would be cutting my own throat."

"I've never known you to be afraid, Bill."

"It's not the kind of fear you think it is," Bill replied without looking into the eyes of his old comrade. "Not the fear of dying. It's the fear of living and having no way of supporting myself, of being whittled down to begging for hand-outs. That's what I fear, and if I was to go up against Lucky and them, well, that's exactly what would happen."

Bill dropped his head even farther down onto his chest, his eyes no longer reading the list of names, no longer remembering what they'd once meant to him, for not a one, he believed, would care for him now if they could see the way he was, how he'd turned out. Besides, women moved on, men tended to linger and overstay their welcome and hang around looking for ghosts where there weren't any.

"My horse is tied up down at the livery," Bill said. "You're welcome to him. Just give the liveryman this." He quickly scribbled a bill of sale and handed it to Cole. In the margin was the name *Sarah*. "Least I can do for you. Now, if you wouldn't mind clearing out before they find you here, I'd appreciate it."

It was troublesome to be sure when old friends let you down, Cole told himself, but then all men aren't the same and all men wouldn't do what he would do.

"Keep your horse, Bill. When I leave, it will be on my own terms and on that midnight flyer, one way or the other."

"I hope it ain't the other," Bill said,

They each nodded, and then Cole passed out of the office again and around the corner, keeping an eye out for those who would come for him. While Bill Hammer went back to scribbling names of lost loves on a stained envelope, he heard the *crack-crack* of two gunshots and the thunder of a shotgun, and closed his eyes.

The first ones Cole encountered were those two waddies who had been in the café earlier. He saw the one but not the other until it was nearly too late, one at the head of the alley and the other at its end. He threw himself to the dirt just as they each fired, and he thought surely when he saw one man fall and heard the other scream that they'd impossibly shot each other.

But it wasn't so, not entirely. One of them had shot the other—the bullet from the one at the head of the alley slammed into his cohort's chest and knocked him flat while that man's shot missed Cole and everything else but a sideboard of a building. But almost immediately the thunderous boom of a shotgun fired by the cook, Peck, nearly cut the standing man in half, his blood and bone painting the walls of the side of the feed store in greasy red splotches.

The killed man never made so much as a sound, death took him that quickly. The partner he'd shot lay squirming like a worm freshly hooked, his heels digging into the dust as he gripped his bloody shirt front.

"Damn! Damn! Damn!" he swore through gritted teeth.

He was still reaching for the revolver that had spilled away from his unclasped fingers when the gunsmith appeared and reached down and picked it up and stuck it inside his own waistband.

"I do believe you still owe me ten dollars on this LeMat," the gunsmith said to the wounded man, "and it does not look as if now you'll be able to pay, so I'm taking back my merchandise."

Peck eased alongside the gunsmith, the twin

barrels of his blaster leaking gray smoke, the steel warm to the touch.

"Mister Peck, I thought I warned you to stay out of this," Cole said, coming up on the pair.

"Yes, sir, you did, but this beats hell out of slinging hash all day."

Cole traded looks with the gunsmith who raised his palms in supplication and said: "I'm just here to watch over my equipage. Perhaps before this day is through I'll have made a small profit on found armaments no longer needed." Then he strode over to the other dead man and took his iron as well.

"You two better clear the street because Lucky will be bringing his boys soon enough and I doubt any of us are going to be so fortunate from here on out."

"They'll come from the Liberty," Peck opined, pointing with his nose.

"I reckon."

"How you aim on taking 'em?"

"Straight on if I can."

Peck shook his head. So did the gunsmith.

"Won't do," said the gunsmith. "You'll be the duck in a barrel."

"Fish you mean?" Cole said.

"All the same thing."

Peck grinned for the tension in him was high and grinning, even at a lame turn of a phrase, helped some. "I was a sniper in the great conflict," the gunsmith said, "and I can get up in the second-story window over the hat shop and have a line of fire up and down the street."

"You sure you want to get involved in this?" Cole asked.

"You was to ask me yesterday, I'd have said no. But Peck is right about standing by again and letting these rabble-rousers have their way. I'm purely sick of it."

Cole nodded and watched the gunsmith lope across the as yet open street and into the hat shop.

"Knowing they'll come from the Liberty," Peck said, "means I should go around and come up from behind them when you get them into the street."

Cole took a deep breath, knowing that some of them were not going to return home after this day, and he hated to be responsible for men he barely knew.

"If it's your choice," he said, "I won't try and stop you."

"My choice was made a moment ago," Peck said, looking down at the dying waddy who had stopped his squirming and now lay breathing his last shallow breaths.

Again Cole nodded. He had no words for such men, only admiration.

"See if you can't hold 'em off till I get around behind them," Peck said, and went down the alley around behind the buildings in the direction of

Karl's Liberty Palace Saloon, past some quarrel-some dogs nosing garbage, and outhouses that caused the air to be rank, and back doors, some still locked because it was too early to be open for business. He went carrying the shotgun in both hands, his head full of glory that might never come except in eulogies over his coffin. He told himself he might not be handsome enough for regular women because of that blind eye, and he might be a hash slinger, and he might be a lot of other things most men would look down upon, but this once he was going to be something—a force to be reckoned with.

Others had heard the brief gunfire that killed the two waddies—the *crack-crack* and *boom*—but most didn't pay much attention. Gunfire in Gun Town was like thunder in a rainstorm, to be expected. Still, some of the curious who weren't yet sleeping in from the previous night's activities had begun drifting out onto the streets to see what the action was about, while the slatterns who were awake began to place bets with each other on who was getting killed.

Upstairs in Karl's Liberty Palace Saloon, Little Eva still maintained a careful watch over Lenora.

"Sounds like maybe Lucky's having a time of it out there," Eva said, unaware that Lucky and several others were yet gathered downstairs in the saloon in order for Lucky to give them a plan.

The men below had looked up when they heard the gunfire, all of them. Gypsy had arrived shortly before with the others Lucky had wanted, the best of the gunfighters in town at present and ones he knew he could rely on to kill for money—the left-handed Lee Reynolds, the lop-eared Hasty Parker, and the scar-faced Tom Mulligan.

"There's five of us," Lucky said to The Gimp. "Plus Harry and Jake you sent out earlier. It ought to be enough to put John Henry under the sod. The thing I want is to be the one who puts the bullet in him . . . so take him alive, if you can."

The rest looked at one another, some sleepy-eyed and others, as usual, churlish.

"Shit, which is it, Lucky, you want him kilt or don't you?" asked Lee Reynolds. He was wearing a cowhide vest with most of the hair worn off.

"Just place your gun in his ear hole if you get the chance, but let me be the one who does him. We clear?" Lucky growled.

They nodded, and Lucky led them out onto the street and toward the sound where they'd heard the gunfire coming from.

Cole had waited, giving the gunsmith and Peck a chance to get into position, then stepped out of the alley and into the street, the coach gun at the ready. He figured it was good for twenty, thirty yards and with a wide spread the farther out they were.

He stood waiting.

Then they came. Four abreast.

What Cole couldn't know was that The Gimp had volunteered to come around the other way to try and get Cole in a crossfire. At least that is what he said he wanted to do. But it wasn't Cole that The Gimp was most interested in killing.

As soon as the others walked out of Karl's Liberty Palace Saloon, The Gimp quick-hopped up the stairs and entered the room where Little Eva held the gun on Lenora. Both women looked up suddenly when The Gimp burst into the room.

"What's going on out there?" Little Eva said. "We heard gunshots. Is Lucky OK?"

"Sure, sure he is," Gypsy said. "You watching her good?" He thrust his chin at Lenora, and when Eva turned to look at her, The Gimp slipped the knife in just under Little Eva's back ribs. She gasped, and he withdrew the blade, and brought it around front and drew it quickly across her throat. She spilled out of her seat, trying to stanch the flush of blood, kicked her tiny feet, and tossed about like a wrecked chicken.

The Gimp wiped the bloody blade on his trouser leg and said—"When this is finished, I'm coming back for you."—and slipped out the door.

For a full moment Lenora did not move. But then she did.

Peck was nearly to the corner of the alley where he planned to turn up—just beyond the back of Karl's Liberty Palace Saloon—when suddenly the rear door opened and he turned, but not in time to stop the bullet from The Gimp's gun that struck him between the eyes—the good one and the bad one. In death's spasm, Peck's fingers squeezed the triggers of the shotgun, blasting both shells into the dirt.

"You dumb son-of-a-bitch," The Gimp said. "You should have stayed slinging hash and telling your stupid war stories."

The Gimp went down the same way that Peck had just come.

Moving toward Cole were four men—Lucky Jack in the middle of them, their guns in their hands, cocked, ready to fire. Cole glanced up at the open window above the hat shop and saw the gunsmith appear, the barrel of his sporting rifle poking through, and felt assured, knowing he was up there. Seconds after he'd entered the hat shop, the owner had come running out like a frightened bird and fled down the street.

Cole waited until the gunslingers got within calling distance, the coach gun at eye level, not that he needed to aim but only show them the twin black holes that could cut loose a hail of buckshot.

"It doesn't have to be this way!" he said.

"I was about to say the same thing to you, John Henry!" Lucky called back.

Beyond the gunslingers Cole could see others coming out unto the street, the curious, the bored. Death in all its manifold forms was an attraction that drew a crowd, like to a hanging or a circus. To witness life snuffed out was the great mystery and everyone wanted in on it, to watch and wonder what became of that which once was a living, breathing man?

"Put away your weapons and we can settle this peaceful!" Lucky called.

They slowly spread apart from one another so that even if Cole pulled both triggers his buckshot wouldn't take them all down at once.

"No matter!" he called to Lucky Jack. "I'll make sure you get both pills!"

"Shit, how'd it ever come to this, you and me, John Henry? What we was, what we are now."

"Reckon it doesn't matter now, does it?"

"No, I reckon it don't."

A moment earlier Lenora had come out of the back of Karl's Liberty Palace Saloon, the pepper-box gun in her fist and nearly stumbled over Peck's body. She could not bear to look into his smashed forehead and caught only the last glimpse of The Gimp farther up the alley and just turning a corner.

Her rage was such she lost all reason. Murder was in her mind and in the air and let murder be as murder would. It was all madness now, the killing, the bloodshed, and she was part of it, too, Lenora told herself. *You were always part of it. You let Lucky steal your heart and your brains and everything else. You let him involve you in murder and you did nothing about it. Do something about it now!*

The Gimp had eased out of the alley and enough into the street to get a view of the broad back of Cole. He smiled slowly as he eased his revolver out of his holster and took aim. He was less than a dozen feet away and the target was going to be the easiest thing he'd ever had to shoot at. He could not miss.

Lucky Jack saw Gypsy, knew that the jig was up for Cole, said out of the side of his mouth: "Boys, when I give the order, cut him down."

Cole's forefinger lay in the curve of the double triggers, the cold steel just waiting for his command.

The Gimp thumbed back the hammer of his single-action, a double click. Just enough to catch Cole's attention, to tell him the secret of the assassin, and he knew it was going to be too late to kill them all. But then he did not have to.

"Now!" Lucky Jack commanded.

Cole tried to escape the bullet from behind by

diving sideways while cutting loose with the coach gun.

He felt the sharp bite of The Gimp's bullet high on his right hip even as he dropped the empty shotgun and rolled away, grabbing now for the Colt riding in his shoulder rig, jerking it free and firing off two quick rounds at the half hidden Gimp.

Wood splintered from a support post and clipped The Gimp's face, drawing a ribbon of blood and leaving him cursing, not sure if he'd been shot or not.

Cole's shotgun blast had killed the man on the end of the line and broken the leg of the man next to him. Both were down, one screaming bloody murder and the other one silent as stone, most of his chest a meaty maw of bone and torn muscle and flesh.

Up in the window, the gunsmith took aim and finished the man with the broken leg, then swung around to take out the other two but both men had run under the overhang just below him. He took a deep breath and let it out, kept the barrel trained on anything in the street, wondering where Peck was, if he was OK. He looked up the street for his friend and did not see him.

The gunfire had caused the spectators to dart back inside whatever doorways they could find.

"That damn' useless Gimp!" Lucky swore as

he and scar-faced Tom Mulligan hovered in the doorway of Church's Jewelry Store.

Across the way Cole had crashed through the doorway of the telegrapher's office. The telegrapher had jumped clean out of his chair, not sure what the gunfire was all about or why his place was being broken into by a man with a gun in his hand and blood wetting his pants leg.

"Don't shoot me, please! I have a wife who is sickly!"

"Get down!" Cole shouted as he took position by the window of cheap glass that caused everything to look watery. He could not draw a bead on either of the two men across the way, hidden as they were by the door frame of the jeweler's. He glanced down at his burning hip, fingered open the tear in his trousers. The bullet had clipped muscle but he wasn't sure if it had lodged in or gone completely through. It burned like blue hell and was numb to the touch, the blood warm and sticky.

Several hot rounds shattered the telegraph office's window glass, giving a clear portal to the outer world.

"Oh dear, oh dear!" the telegrapher moaned from his position face down on the floor. "They're going to kill us all."

CHAPTER TWENTY-FOUR

Over in his office Bill Hammer listened to the gunfire, reached for his bottle, and poured himself a glass of the tanglefoot, downed it, then poured another. *You should get out there and do the right thing, like you always did,* he told himself. *I can't.* More gunfire, another drink. *Sometimes these things just have to work themselves out, you know that. No one man can save the world from the savages and ravages. Ask ol' Jesus. He tried, and look where it got him. It'll be over soon, then you can go out and help clean up the garbage, like you've always done. Do Lucky's bidding, like you been doing. You're bought and paid for . . . bought and paid for.*

He poured another. Drank it more slowly this time.

Gypsy Flynn was still clutching his bloody face when Lenora spoke his name.

"What's the matter, Gimp, you get hurt?"

He wiped blood out of his eye, spun around, and saw her standing there.

"I've come to be with you, darling," she said. Then she shot him through the neck and watched him do a two-step as if demonstrating how to dance, a spout of blood shooting from his neck wound. She stood watching and listening to the gurgling sounds coming from him as he slowly gave up the dance and sank to his knees, his face a ghastly mask of pain and disbelief.

"What's that you say, you half-footed little bastard?"

His hands were wrapped around his throat as if to hold the blood in but that was like trying to stop a busted water pipe. He could not speak, or protest the pain and fear that had welled up in him, for strangulation by one's own blood would be indescribable even if one had time to try. The Gimp did not have the luxury of time. Blood spilled from his mouth when he opened it as if to speak.

"I'm sorry, lover," she said. "I just can't quite understand you."

His eyes grew large, bulged as he struggled to keep on his knees, his small hard frame jerking as he strove to suck in one small bit of air into his lungs. But the passageway was blocked, clotted with too much blood, and the drowning was nearly complete.

"Oh, I suppose I should take a bit of pity, even on you, Gimp," she said. "Though really, no one would blame me if I didn't, after what you did to me. But I am, after all, a woman and we both know how we women are weak and the fairer sex and pity even rabid animals. So here is my gift to you, dear."

She pulled the trigger on the pepperbox gun again and again until it clicked on empty chambers and still the little man did not die completely. He lay twitching.

She shook her head. "Not quite dead, not alive. It must feel like hell."

Then she walked away into the maze of alleyways.

"Go get some more men," Lucky ordered Mulligan.

"I step out into that street he's going to gun me down."

"If you don't step out into that street, *I'm* going to gun you down," Lucky said, poking the muzzle of his revolver into Mulligan's ribs."

The bone-white scar that ran the length of Mulligan's face from ear tip to the bottom of his jaw glistened with sweat. "It ain't right, Lucky. It's suicide you're asking."

"Don't worry, you do this and I'll make you my right-hand man and add a hundred dollars to your pockets."

What choice have I got? Mulligan asked himself, and darted into the street hoping to get across it without ending up in perdition. But he did not see nor was he aware or would he ever have considered the front sight of Abe Adelmann's sporting rifle poking through the upper window of the hat shop where he once went to buy a jolly whore a fine feathered hat. No, he did not even catch a glimpse of the barrel of the gun as it followed him, and then spat fire.

The bullet shattered his spine and for a brief second Mulligan wondered what happened to his legs. It was as though a scythe had suddenly cut them from under him. He lay, chuffing in the street. He tried to move his legs but they did not move. He tried to move his arms, but they didn't move, either. Nothing moved. His breathing grew hard. "Oh, what a terrible thing this is," he muttered, then closed his eyes and slipped away to that unknown place where the dead go.

Lucky Jack saw Mulligan get cut down. "Son-of-a-bitch!"

He knew he had enemies in town, rivals who would try and take him out, and that is what he figured was happening. The only way to get control was to show everyone he was still the man to be reckoned with. But he never reckoned that even in the worst towns there were yet a few good people.

He called across the way: "John Henry!"

Cole said nothing, still trying to get a glimpse of Lucky, hidden in the doorway.

"John Henry! I've an offer to make you."

Cole remained silent.

"One of us is going to die today. You or me. We both know it. So here's the thing. Let's do it as men and not assassins. We had a code once, men like us. I'm ready to live by it again . . . or die by it. My men are dead. I know you got a gun up in that window. He just killed Mulligan. You call him off and you and me will meet in the street and do it like they used to do it." He laughed. "Well, like they have us doing it in those dime novels. Face to face, man to man. Best man wins and the other gets buried."

Cole knew if he were to agree, it would take considerable luck to come out on top because he'd seen Lucky in action before and there was every chance Lucky would come out on top this time. But he also knew that Lucky had always been a man of his word and would not play it underhanded.

"What'll you say, John Henry?"

One way or the other he was going to have to fight, Cole told himself, and maybe this was the best way. Just end it. He could stay put and maybe bleed to death—his boot was filling up with blood—or . . . "Let me see you!" he called.

Lucky Jack holstered his gun and stepped far enough out of the doorway for Cole to see him but not far enough to be shot from the window above.

"Stay put," Cole said to the telegrapher.

"You're preaching to the choir," the telegrapher said.

Cole came out of the telegraph office, hoping his shot hip would support him. He glanced up at the window across the street and waved off the gunsmith who withdrew the barrel of his target gun.

"We're clear!" he called to Lucky. "It's just me and you."

Lucky stepped farther out of the doorway and down into the hardpan of the street. They stood about fifteen feet apart, maybe twenty, the sun at Lucky Jack's back and Cole squinting into it.

"We can still square the deal," Cole said. "You just turn over the woman and let us ride out on the night flyer."

"Nah, I don't think I can do that. You know how much I hate losing at anything."

"I know she threw in with you," Cole said. "I know the whole story. She told it to me."

"Then why the hell you want to take her back to that old man?"

"Because he hired me to."

"That's just being damn' stupid and damn' stubborn," Lucky replied.

"Maybe so."

From the upper window the gunsmith watched, fixated on the scene below. Men did not normally kill each other with such formality—face to face on a wide-open street in the middle of the morning.

He held the rifle's barrel with both hands, his cheek leaning against the cold blue steel. It was of no comfort to him.

The gunfighters were tense as coiled rattlers—their strike unknowable until it happened. It was as if they each could sense the other's heart beating. And then it happened. Two hands moving swiftly, raising their revolvers that were already in hand and the difference in speed was at that point negligible because they hadn't had to draw from holsters. It was all about coolness in the face of death, all about steadiness and lack of fear, and one man had it a half-degree more than the other man. Both revolvers fired almost as if one. One man's bullet missed by an inch and the other's slammed home, right through the breastbone.

The gunsmith from his perch saw a piece of white linen shred as John Henry's round struck Lucky Jack's clean linen shirt. He saw the man stagger backward and look down at himself, the spread of blood staining that lovely white shirt. He saw how Lucky Jack clutched himself and turned around as if he'd forgotten something back at Karl's Liberty Palace Saloon, something precious that he needed to retrieve, and then take two more steps and fall face down with the weight of a stone toppling, and lay still.

A pallor of gunsmoke held in the air between the two men—the one living and the other dead—a cloud that slowly dissipated, like the blood that pooled into the street beneath the body of Lucky Jack, and would be all but forgotten with little trace in time to come.

For a moment longer Cole stood, staring at the man he'd just killed, wondering why it had to have been this way when there were a thousand other ways it could have been. Then he holstered his gun and sat down on the walk, feeling a bit woozy from loss of blood.

Someone went and got the doctor, Pursewater, who came right away with his medical bag, bandages, tools, and set to work on Cole's wound with forceps and needle and thread while Cole made himself a cigarette and smoked it.

Somebody brought a bottle of whiskey and handed it to Cole, and he took a drink, and then another.

Others gathered, too, to visit the death scene, the whores dipping hankies in the blood of the deceased, and some laughing as they did so.

The last to come was old Bill Hammer, walking up the street slowly, wearily, his hand resting on the butt of his gun, a gun that hadn't been fired in years. He surveyed the carnage, then walked over to where Cole sat, a bottle in one hand, a cigarette in the other.

"Well, I reckon it's over," he said dejectedly as if he himself had been part of the battle.

Cole looked up at him. "Go and bury your dead, Bill."

CHAPTER TWENTY-FIVE

Later, John Henry Cole heard the night flyer's whistle shrieking in the darkness like a woman who'd lost her children—a long, lonesome sound. Cole gathered himself and limped to the station where he waited until the miniature moon of light appeared around a curve in the great blackness, a most welcome sight.

"Here comes your train, Mister Cole," the station agent said with new respect. By now everyone in town knew his name.

Cole stood and waited for the lumbering beast of an engine to come to a halt, then walked through its chuffing steam to a passenger car and climbed aboard.

Twenty minutes later the train pulled out, and Cole leaned back in his seat and silently thanked the man who'd given him the bottle of tanglefoot to help kill the pain in his leg. He smiled a soft weak smile. *At least my head don't hurt so much, any more.*

The liveryman offered Rita May and Kate $125 for the medicine wagon, lock, no stock, and barrel, including the remaining cases of patent medicine. They readily agreed and caught the next westbound flyer, figuring San Francisco was probably the most likely place for a couple of enterprising independent women.

"Do you think we'll do well?" Kate asked.

"I think we could always do worse," Rita May said.

They held hands. The train carried them away.

Lenora Wilson disappeared and was never heard from again, although it was quite possible that she changed her name and became a new person with a new life in a new place, with new dreams and hopes and possibly schemes. But she could have as likely joined a religious order—which was fashionable for wayward women with lost souls.

Wilson died the very morning that his younger son arrived in Red Pony to take charge of the body of his brother.

The young town marshal wasn't any older than Bo Wilson had been. Jesse took stock of him.

"You Indian?"

"Half," Tom said.

"Tom Moon . . . that sounds Indian."

"My mother was. My father is Scots-English."

Tom took Jesse over to the undertaker's where Bo's body had been kept cold with blocks of dry ice packed around the body inside a lead-lined coffin.

Bo's color was that of blue chalk, his lips darker, nearly black.

"Sign here to claim the body and he's yours,"

Tom said, handing a piece of paper to Jesse along with a stub of a pencil. He watched as the form was signed.

"I'll have your brother's coffin taken over to the train," Tom said.

"I always knew it would come to this," Jesse said sadly.

The two of them went to the train station where Tom had some men go and get the coffin and deliver it on a handcart, from which it would be slid into a railway baggage car.

Jesse, not yet aware of his father's passing that morning, toed the dirt with his boot, his thumbs hitched in the pockets of his waistcoat. "It all seems such a waste, don't it?"

"How's that?"

"Life, everything, I don't know."

"I reckon we get what we deserve," Tom said.

The conductor announced the boarding.

"You remind me of someone, but I can't say who," Jesse said.

"I get that a lot," Tom said.

He had received a telegram late last evening.

Tom. Leaving for home on midnight flyer. STOP. Will arrive in three days. STOP. Let Woman know. STOP. JHC.

He took out the telegram, read it again, balled it in his fist, and dropped it onto the ground.

Then he turned and walked away.

ABOUT THE AUTHOR

Bill Brooks is the author of numerous novels of historical and frontier fiction. After a lifetime of working a variety of jobs, from shoe salesman to shipyard worker, Brooks entered the health care profession where he was in management for sixteen years before turning to his first love—writing. Once he decided to turn his attention to becoming a published writer, Brooks worked several more odd jobs to sustain himself, including wildlife tour guide in Sedona, Arizona where he lived and became even more enamored with the West of his childhood heroes, Roy Rogers and Gene Autry. Brooks wrote a string of frontier fiction novels, beginning with *The Badmen* (1992) and *Buscadero* (1993), before he attempted something more lyrical and literary in the critically acclaimed: *The Stone Garden: The Epic Life of Billy the Kid* (2002). This was followed in succession by *Pretty Boy: The Epic Life of Pretty Boy Floyd* (2003) and *Bonnie & Clyde: A Love Story* (2005). *The Stone Garden* was named by *Booklist* as one of the top ten Westerns of the decade. After that trio of novels, Brooks was asked to return to frontier fiction by an editor who had moved to a new publisher and he wrote in succession three series for them, beginning with *Law For Hire* (2003), then *Dakota Lawman* (2005), and finishing up with *The Journey of Jim Glass* (2007). *The Messenger* (Five Star, 2009) was Brooks's twenty-second novel. *Blood Storm* (Five Star, 2011) was the first novel in a series of John Henry Cole adventures. It was praised by *Publishers Weekly* as a well-crafted story with an added depth due to its characters. *Booklist* said of *Winter Kill* (Five Star, 2013), the third John Henry Cole story: "Western fans are largely forced to survive on reprints originally published decades ago, which makes the work of contemporary writers like Brooks, who haven't abandoned the grand Western tradition, all the more satisfying." Bill Brooks now lives in northeast Indiana.

| Books are produced in the United States using U.S.-based materials | Books are printed using a revolutionary new process called THINKtech™ that lowers energy usage by 70% and increases overall quality | Books are durable and flexible because of Smyth-sewing | Paper is sourced using environmentally responsible foresting methods and the paper is acid-free |

Center Point Large Print
600 Brooks Road / PO Box 1
Thorndike, ME 04986-0001 USA

(207) 568-3717

US & Canada:
1 800 929-9108
www.centerpointlargeprint.com